Nothing but Waves and Wind

Christine Montalbetti

NOTHING BUT WAVES AND WIND

Translated from the French by Jane Kuntz

DALKEY ARCHIVE PRESS

Despite its mission to support French literature in translation, and in particular to to support the cause and well-being of translators, CNL (Centre national du livre) would not provide support for the translator of this book, and this at a time when there has been a substantial decrease in the number of books being translated into English. Dalkey Archive urges CNL to return to its mission of aiding translators.

Originally published in French by P.O.L. as *Plus rien que les vagues et le vent* in 2014.

Library of Congress Cataloging-in-Publication Data
Names: Montalbetti, Christine, author. | Kuntz, Jane, translator.
Title: Nothing but waves and wind / Christine Montalbetti ; translated by Jane Kuntz.
Other titles: Plus rien que les vagues et le vent. English
Description: First Dalkey archive edition. | Victoria, TX : Dalkey Archive Press, 2017.
Identifiers: LCCN 2017005012 | ISBN 9781943150182 (pbk. : acid-free paper)
Classification: LCC PQ2713.O576 P5813 2017 | DDC 843/.92--dc23
LC record available at https://lccn.loc.gov/2017005012

www.dalkeyarchive.com
Victoria, TX / McLean, IL / Dublin

Dalkey Archive Press publications are, in part, made possible through the support of the University of Houston-Victoria and its programs in creative writing, publishing, and translation.

Printed on permanent/durable acid-free paper.

For sure, this story has been brewing in my head for days, and it can wake me up out of a dead sleep.

It's like one of those animals that take up residence in your home, become a fixture, like that owl you hear scratching around in your attic, a bat flapping against the inside surface of your chimney every night, an inadvertently sidetracked field mouse so nimble that you've given up trying to trap it, as it furtively goes about committing its little misdemeanors around your house.

Or rather, what I should say is that it's more like the ocean, like the tide that comes in below my window and gathers up all the ill waves, then tosses them right back onto the pale, helpless beach: the story overwhelms me, then recedes, leaving me a short respite, then surges back with equal vigor, an obstinate pounding.

But whichever way I tell it, I'll have to talk sooner or later about Colter and the others. I'll have to tell you about Moses, Harry Dean, and the murky business involving Shannon. And about other things, too, having to do with Wendy, and Perry, and even little Mary. And of course, at some point, I'll tell you about McCain. Since there was this guy McCain.

In all this, though, what you really need to do above all else is to hear the ocean.

The ocean that was already there, beating against the shore, so much more than mere background, a furious, uncontrollable presence, an endless display of unfathomable anger. And what that did to them, to Colter and the others, that's also something I need to tell.

Because against that, they were powerless, against the sheer force of the ocean, the way it weirdly modeled their behavior, its insidiously contagious influence.

The same ocean outside my bay window that continuously undermines the shore, swallowing up the sand beneath, retreating to catch its breath, then surges forward with still greater force, unforgiving, to strike the coastline again and again, never wondering why it does what it does.

In the Night

IN THE NIGHT, the outside world loses the daylight color that makes it recognizable and civilized. It becomes terra incognita, where we move blindly forward into silences and sounds, our useless eyes wide open, all our senses on the alert. The world is full of invisible dangers—cracked sidewalks, protruding tree roots—things that our feet would instinctively avoid by day, and we are suddenly in the grip of a single thought, the possibility that something is about to emerge from the shadows, something alive that we fear is poised to pounce (the pulse quickens, the mind races). All this makes walking by night an intensely unpleasant experience. Darkness annuls the very idea of landscape. You sense depth and relief in the abstract only, you hear, smell and touch, but the visual field is gone. The outdoors, having lost all points of reference, is nothing but a kind of abyss. We are isolated bodies moving as best we can through the valley of darkness.

Walking home from Moses's bar, I would occasionally follow a coastal path that a row of trees separated from the water's edge. Sometimes, the moon would cast its white glow on the ocean, silhouetting the pines that twisted up from the beach. But more often, the sky was thick with clouds that devoured the moon, a flat, inky sky that absorbed everything. I could hear the ocean breathing, the liquid sound of waves excited by their own dogged determination. The treetops trembled overhead.

But as a rule, I took the main street, and roused the dogs that would bark from behind fences as I walked past. I wondered whether they were barking instinctively or for some other reason, if they had actually interiorized the notion that it was their duty to guard the house, with its little yard plunged into darkness.

There were times when I wouldn't head right home after leaving the bar. I would sit on the front stoop just long enough to get my thoughts in order.

What was I thinking back then? Nothing in particular, I guess. A chaotic mix of opposing sensations that I surrendered to, waiting for them to subside and vanish. Was there any hint as to what was to come? Probably, on occasion, but so mixed up with the rest that they got lost in the flow of nebulous thoughts that took advantage of my inebriated state to flood my mind all at once.

Because it's true, I could have anticipated how things were going to turn out. Maybe even taken some precautions, and who knows, avoided the worst. But I didn't see it coming, none of it. I just sat out in front of Moses's bar, letting the night wash over me, in the hope that the wind would slap me around and sober me up.

How many times did I sit outside that bar with nothing but the night all around?

Out there somewhere, the ocean was heaving its noisy mass of unfriendly surf.

My memory of those last months is now a muddy magma, molten and confused, but the first time I entered Moses's bar, that much I remember like it was yesterday. Moses (whose name I hadn't learned yet) wiping his beer mugs, and behind him, that framed photograph. But I'll get to that later.

What I saw that first night, as I entered the dimly lit, musty locale, its stale air heavy with spume, were three backs hunched over the bar, perched on stools. Three backs that could have been anybody, any guys on barstools in those plaid shirts and down jackets that everyone around here wears; still, they reminded me of something, I was sure of it.

They didn't turn around, but must have felt something happening behind them: my hesitation, the slow grind of hinges told them that whoever just came through the door wasn't from around these parts. I stepped softly, as if to defuse the tension that their motionlessness and sudden silence inflicted on the room. By the time I reached the bar, they turned to have a look, and I exchanged glances with each one in turn: I recognized them instantly.

I might as well go ahead and tell you it was at the Blueberry Inn that I'd first seen them, two or three days earlier. The Blueberry, in case you're wondering, is an inn located a bit inland, about a half hour's drive from Moses's place, surrounded by forest. I stopped there by chance—not knowing then how much this place would matter in my story—on the road that led here from Long Beach. So I should back up a bit, so that you'll understand how it all started at the Blueberry. Or even the day before I got to the Blueberry, along a certain stretch of Long Beach where things really began with the pelicans, which I should have mentioned from the very start.

Pelican Bay

IF YOU COULD see those pelicans hovering over the ocean, on the lookout for fish below the roiling water, how they were able to spot them somehow beneath the churning waves and then dive, their long, pointy beaks aimed straight down, looking so weapon-like, a pair of pincers that would seize their prey with painstaking precision.

They'd wait to resurface before swallowing their catch. The fish must still have been wriggling in the pelicans' gullets as they contorted their necks to gulp down their meal, all fresh and bathed in salt water. After which, they would just bob around, eyes on the horizon, rocked by the wavelets, before once again taking to the air.

Poured into their skin-tight neoprene wetsuits, the surfers (I'm talking about California here, folks) were paddling among the birds, indifferent to the ongoing butchery all around them, waiting for the next wave, eyes glued to water's movement.

What could one read in those eyes? Vigilance, yes, but I'd also say an uncanny composure, as if all thought were suspended, blanked, the touch of despondency that sets in during a lull in the action, when the waves fail to build. But when they did, the surfers were often overcome, suddenly tossed into the water, laid low with outrageous ease (yes, outrage hit them head on, outrage and spume). While upending the riders, the wave would suck the board under, causing it to disappear for a time. The surfer would resurface, feverishly blinking his salt-stung eyes, then finally catch sight of the missing board rolling with the swell at some distance, bobbing uselessly among the pelicans as they carried on their massacre.

No matter which way I present the story, it had to start with the pelicans, because, when I look back on it now, they seem to set the tone.

If you drive a little further north, those dive-bombing brutes are replaced entirely by seagulls, crisscrossing the sky or cakewalking along the sand. And that's where I was headed. I left the pelican beach in the early afternoon. From Long Beach, you take Chestnut Avenue, nothing to it, all the way to West Shoreline. I kept on I-710 for a few minutes, as instructed by my GPS (turn left onto I-405, she crooned) and continued for about forty-five minutes. I did what I was told, putting up no resistance, happily submissive. I found the female voice hypnotizing, and my body fell into step with her commands. I then got on Highway 5. On the screen, an arrow moving smoothly up a groove provided graphic proof of my progress.

Automatic transmission, speed limit fifty-five: the landscape rolled by uneventfully, that's what I recall. Inside the car, silence and a sense of slow motion. After the pelican beach, everything here felt unexpectedly gentle.

I took a couple of cat naps in gas station parking lots, absorbed a few triangular sandwiches, purchased a large coffee at every stop, placing it in the little ring designed for that purpose, and drove on, sipping the brew as it cooled.

Was I thinking about anything in particular? No, not really.

I got off Highway 5 some twenty hours later, late morning, and just outside Portland, I started heading for the coast. It had begun to rain, a fine drizzle speckling my windshield. The wipers swept back and forth, unhurriedly, leaving the droplets time to gather before wiping them away again, in an endless pendulum swing.

It starts out like a road story, now that I think of it.

I arrived on a rainy day in a rented Ford (a white Crown

Victoria, rear-wheel drive). With the cruise control set, the car
gobbled up the miles all by itself—it did quite well without
me—while I contemplated the pearls of rain as they formed and
disappeared, fresh droplets like a new morning, massacred once
again, annihilated by the rubber blade that the wipers pressed
to the glass. This went on for a while, this seesaw battle in the
foreground: raindrops are erased then make a bold comeback,
extinction and rebirth in a steady, continuous motion, wipers
versus showers, with each one by turns ceding victory to the
other.

Then I stopped one last time before getting to the ocean.

So here we are, at the Blueberry Inn, as you can see from the
painted sign at the entrance to the parking area.

See me park my Ford in front of the bay windows, get out
and lock the vehicle remotely, not with the casual air of one
who's come to expect obedience, but with a certain satisfaction
and surprise (don't know about you, but I always get a kick
out of that amazing power to command things at a distance,
without touching them).

After so many hours on the road, I'm wobbly on my feet,
like standing on a boat deck.

I'm at first reluctant to enter through a white fiberboard
door (probably an emergency exit), but I do anyway, and burst
right into the bar. A TV screen is showing an endless loop of
footage of rival fans brawling in the bleachers at some sports
event, scenes of total anarchy (the injured are being taken out
on stretchers); three regulars at the bar are mesmerized, staring
up at the camera's tight shots of these angry men, and seeing in
them their secret selves.

You could tell that these three would not be averse to a good
scuffle; and their overly demonstrative astonishment (or at least,
that's what they were saying, what they were at great pains to be
seeming to say) at such senseless violence (every time the aging

waitress passed, they pretended to share her concern) was mixed with a secret desire, a muzzled, repressed urge, jealousy tinged with regret at not being there at the stadium, in the stands, to lend a helping hand. They would have been hard-pressed to explain that sometimes you need to feel another person's weight against yours, to measure it against your own, however frenetically.

The aging waitress (Wendy, according to the badge she wore pinned to her maroon uniform) wasn't fooled, but these were paying customers, without whom the bar would have little to show for itself, deserted because she couldn't keep her opinions to herself. So, she stifled her suspicion, pretending that they all agreed it was a scandal.

I went and sat down a little further away, in the restaurant area, burgundy carpet, wide-angle windows looking onto the parking lot. There was my Ford, which in a little while would greet me with blinking headlights, as if my return were a cause for rejoicing (how does the heart not melt at these signs of gratitude which the vehicle—like dogs kept on a leash in front of a supermarket that yip with joy when at last their master emerges from the store after an anxious wait—demonstrates in a manner so frank and direct, so disarmingly ingenuous?).

It was that same Wendy, whose rough voice seemed synonymous with efficiency, as if her gruffness itself was what got things moving, who took my order for a chiliburger. I turned to my right and looked for a moment at the dreary gray outdoors, a view truncated by the vase of artificial flowers on the windowsill: a blacktopped area, fringed on the other side of the road by a row of cylindrical mailboxes that suggested there must be people living somewhere back behind those trees, houses nestled at the end of some hypothetical road, invisible from where I sat.

I thought again of the pelicans.

Those ruthless birds tearing through the seascape with complete impunity, it occurs to me now that they were giving me a kind of warning. But of course, they couldn't have cared less about warning me about anything; they just went about their business. Still, without knowing it, they were showing me how things worked on this coast. Just an idea I had, and later forgot.

Wendy returned with my chiliburger, and I began eating. The slanted light brought the red beans into relief, overexposing the occasional bit of grated cheese or causing a translucent onion to glow.

The three sports fiends at the bar still had their eyes glued to the screen, where some game was now in progress.

Those three guys, how could I have guessed that I'd be seeing them again?

I got back in the car and drove out to the ocean.

It was raining again, but a rain that was somehow shot through with light. The late afternoon had taken on pastel shades but with bright accents. The vast sky's reflection into the ocean nearby lent something surprisingly limpid to the soft blandness of the waning colors.

The motel was easy to spot, though.

The dark mass back-lit by the ocean, the arrangement of its low-slung buildings. Something about its presence immediately attracted me. I drove around a bit, just to get a feel for the surroundings. As I drove along the main road, every perpendicular street on my right led straight to the shore, while on the left, there were houses set into yards. On the way back, I got onto a road that tracked the shore, all bumpy and potholed, from which I could make out a few shacks built right on the beach's edge, some of them flanked by twisted trees whose horrifying silhouette, seemingly frozen in a moment of terror on some stormy night, strongly evoked the notion of torment.

The road got me back to the motel. I parked in front of the main building and opened the car door to the roar of the waves nearby. The sound poured into the cabin, and like lassos roping their prey, pulled me out of the car.

The motel sign titled the scene: *The Waves.*

In the wood-sided shack that served as the reception, behind a makeshift desk, a pasty, rotund man came out from a back room and had me fill out a form. *Yes, one night only.* I checked the box.

Months later, I'm still here.

Ulysses Returns

WELL, YOU COULD never accuse *The Waves* of false publicity, since waves are just about all you can see from the picture windows in the rooms, that ocean, so enormous, so exhausted by its labors, heaving its considerable mass, then collapsing along its vast lateral expanse, over and over and over, under the swollen sky. Now it retreats, finally giving up, you might think, but only to regroup and surge back even stronger, angrier, and pummel the beach more furiously. Listen to the equivocal ebbing, it murmurs to us: we get what we deserve.

We never spoke of it since, but I'm sure those three guys at Moses's place saw me enter the Blueberry Inn, a few days earlier, when I'd stopped to try their local specialty, and gazed through the bay window at this fragment of America. I even think I can safely say that on that day at the Blueberry Inn, the kind of hostility they naturally felt toward any stranger who set foot on their territory must have been intensified by the sportscast replay of those fight scenes at the stadium, by the spectacle of the rescuers pushing their way through the crowd (with that serious look, you know the one, of concern and responsibility) and the injured bodies being tossed onto stretchers and loaded into ambulances (unless you've been involved firsthand, you have no idea how rude rescue teams can be).

And that's what I felt that first night at Moses's place, that somehow my face reminded them of those bruised bodies, brought back the memory of their own underhanded reaction to the scenes on the screen, as they pretended, whenever the old waitress walked past (Wendy, yes, I can call her Wendy), to protest that such behavior did a disservice to the sport, where in fact, they enjoyed every blow, as if they were the ones throwing the punches.

Amidst all this uneasiness, that first night at Moses's, I never flinched. I ordered a beer, and stood at the bar, right next to them, as if I'd always been there.

While I was drinking, having a second and even a third so it didn't look like I was trying to slink away, it's quite possible, I had plenty of time to imagine (yes, this is what was going through my mind at the time) the scene of an ordinary lynching in this little town of Cannon Beach, where not a whole lot happens, especially in the off-season, which it was then. And where you had to deal with the fury of the waves and those cold winds that whipped and twisted the trees into submission. That's what I was thinking, it came to me on the spot (imagination can get the best of you, I thought then; well, actually, not right then and there at Moses's bar, where I was letting my thoughts meander to the point where I almost believed them, but later on, when I thought back on the whole scene, with a few weeks' hindsight, by which time I felt like I was getting to know this little crowd), that this particular night, under a starless sky, because of the violence of the ocean nearby that might easily infect them, because of everything that was roiling inside them, behind those expressionless faces, that's what I thought to myself, that their general discontent could have found expression all of a sudden in a useless barroom brawl, in which my sole offense would have been that I was an outsider.

But they simply ignored me, for they knew that it was exactly that, a second exchange of glances that was to be avoided at all costs to keep things from turning sour. So I just stood there and drank my three beers, the air thick with the hostility of their three pigheaded profiles that refused to look my way.

Still, I came back.

Night after night, we got to know each other.

They were Colter, Shannon, and Harry Dean, in case I wanted to know. We shook hands.

You could say that the three of them made a good team, with personalities both compatible and different, as is usually the case.

Harry Dean lived inland, not far from the Blueberry Inn, on a farm where he worked. Puny as he was, you had a hard time imagining him wielding a pitchfork at the crack of dawn, hauling buckets, wading through the mud and muck in rubber boots that must have gaped around his skinny calves. But he was clearly getting the job done, or he'd never have lasted that long. At nightfall, he'd have himself a ciggy and watch the sky change color, then he'd take the old pickup that sat idle in the barn and go pick up Colter, who had a room at the Blueberry. And they'd go down to Moses's bar, taking the road that cut through the woods.

There were times during the year when nature did its work on its own, germinating without his help, down under the layer of frost; that's when you could find Harry spending nearly all day at the Blueberry with Colter, and Shannon would come join them there. That's how I saw them at the Blueberry. And that's how I saw them at Moses's place, almost every night, because almost every night, that's where they went, the two that came down, and Shannon, who lived here in Cannon Beach with little Mary.

Every so often, there was a fourth. Tim Doyle, the guy who ran the souvenir shop, would sometimes show up. Or on rare occasions, the duo Harper and Marvin, who were truck drivers. Those two were always on the road, but whenever a trip took them anywhere near Cannon Beach, they'd make a detour to stop off at Moses's. They had their shtick down pretty well, one skinny, the other heavyset, the classic comedy duo, the absentminded dreamer and the garrulous extrovert; they knew all the moves. And yeah, sometimes there'd be a surprise guest or two. But when it came right down to it, the true regulars at Moses's bar were the three guys from the Blueberry Inn, none other than, if you don't mind a little revision, a review of the names, Colter, Shannon, and Harry Dean.

Behind the bar, Moses would be washing his glasses, holding one up to the ceiling light from time to time to check for spots. He looked like a loner, cut off from us by the borderline of his bar, enclosed in thoughts we knew nothing about. But he wasn't entirely alone: next to him, a photograph I mentioned in passing but without details, the one of Moses as a child. Moses B. Reed, it says in bold letters, in case you saw absolutely no connection between the scrawny kid in the picture and the grown-up version.

Why did you put that photo there, Moses, is the question I asked myself every time I sat at that bar, I swear; not a single time did that question not go through my mind. What's striking about the photo is the facial expression, the smile that doesn't match the look of terror in the eyes. It was the uncertainty in this face, the fear so legible, and the mouth putting up a brave front. At any rate, the child with the inscrutable smile stuck to Moses like glue. They formed a pair, adult and child, one moving around in 3D and the other necessarily immobile, flat as a flounder, in numbing black and white, but who you'd swear was about to speak his mind, eyes wide open, not missing a scrap of what was happening in the room.

What you could see, after a few pints, was bodies beginning to stutter, needing to take several stabs at each move, lurching to get there. At some point, Moses's place started to feel like the bridge of a ship in a squall. We would sway, coming down hard on a heel for balance all of a sudden, eyes fixed on some vague horizon, some distant line obscured by the swell, some course to be stayed at all costs.

That's how it felt after a while, that's it exactly, as if we were all aboard a ship in rough seas. Bodies starting to sense the roll and trying to keep their queasy balance. Occasionally, someone would actually fall down, and would lie sprawled, all surprised to find himself on the floor, as if he hadn't felt the surge smack the hull of the foundering ship unable to roll with waves. The others would grab him by the armpits and lift him to his feet, even though they were feeling a little seasick themselves, shoulder to shoulder to weather the storm. When folks saw us pitch and roll like that, they could almost imagine the mounting storm clouds, hear the wind gusting, feel its rip. By the end, the place had the atmosphere of a maritime novel, an epic journey over a wild ocean. When Moses named his bar *Ulysses Returns*, maybe that's what he had in mind, because at some point, a bar is like a sinking ship, with bodies hanging on to the counter the way you would to a ship's rail, a trunk, a lifeboat, sailors in a storm, shaky on their pins.

So that you can better picture the barroom itself: wood plank walls, only one window, always shuttered and covered with the standard red and white checkered curtains. Overhead, the ceiling light casts a stingy, yellowish wash of gummy photons onto a couple of tables, usually empty, and a few chairs; photons dragging their feet, barely making it over to the barstools and counter, where what's left of its feeble glow reflects up into the faces of the clients from below (weirdly deforming their profiles), before plunging behind the bar into bottomless darkness, revealing on its way the photograph of the child that remains uncannily visible in the half-light.

Colter's Story

THERE ARE TIMES when I manage to convince myself that the whole thing was basically just a nightmare, and for a while, I actually believe it: the story floats above me like a daydream, a phantasmagoria, the murky residue of a hallucination that haunts the room a while before disappearing altogether. But then, something inside me—a bitter certainty, a gnawing sensation left by this wound—reminds me that it is all too real.

What concerns me, then, what I often wonder, is whether I might have been able to see it coming. There were plenty of signs, you might say. Did I just prefer not to see them?

The fact is that, little by little, with this little Cannon Beach bunch, I was starting to get my bearings.

At first, I went out almost daily.

During daylight hours, sometimes, just to see how I measured up to the great outdoors, I'd go walk the tempestuously powerful space of the beach, and I'll be damned if it wasn't like getting punched in the face when the wind hits you head-on and you have to struggle to keep walking, tightening your muscles against the gusts, your ears battered by the roar of the waves.

But more often, I went out at night, over to the *Ulysses Returns*, where I learned something new each time about Colter and the others, deluding myself into thinking that a kind of gruff friendship might be developing between us.

These guys could talk a lot of hogwash once the beer had warmed them up, most of which was definitely not for all ears. A listener, that's what I was at Moses's place. For them, I was a fresh pair of ears ready to be stuffed with all sorts of tales, and that's exactly what they must have been thinking when they saw me come back to Moses's bar: this guy could play a role in this thing, and in the dim light of the bar, they looked straight into my ear canal, as if it were a hoop through which they'd soon be aiming their shots.

And that's what they did.

They poured all kinds of stuff into my novice ears. I knew that barstool confessions were never aimed at anyone in particular. That the guy on the receiving end is a kind of emissary, an everyman, a vague stand-in for the human race. That's what I must have been for them, the new ambassador, entirely interchangeable with any other. But stories heard are ties that bind, in a way. Night after night, they spun their life stories; and night after night, I felt the bond tighten with every tale they told.

Of all these guys, undoubtedly the most complete story, the one I came to know best, was Colter's story.

Colter's story, I could tell it to you in order, starting with his childhood (which I will get to, his childhood, that is, but Colter himself didn't talk about it until much later), but the easiest way is to start with the house.

Because there was a time when Colter actually had one, the little house with a flower garden that had seemed for so long beyond his reach, something he wouldn't have ever even dreamt of owning. He could describe it to you for hours, it made him so happy, so proud. The façade, Colter would explain, on evenings when he wanted us all to picture it, oh those glorious days of home ownership beneath the vast sky, it was a façade with pediments, you see. One pediment topped the front entrance, and the door was painted hunter green and right in the middle—and this is the icing on the cake—a shiny brass knocker. A second pediment crowned the living room window, a bow window that looked out onto a patch of lawn and a kind of shrub that he'd prune on weekends. His wife (another mirage that had come true) hung flouncy flowered curtains tied back on either side. Their curvy silhouette was visible from the street, which was the main idea, that people passing by would imagine how cozy the place was inside, how well-kept, how comfortable.

The two little pediments (over the front door and window) were echoed by the more imposing triangular shape of the roof, also designed like a pediment (a kind of papa pediment, watching over his little ones), but more solemnly majestic than the other two, set against the sky that, unfortunately, was crisscrossed by those inescapable power lines stretching from one pole to the next; but the view didn't suffer, thought Colter, because they made a musical staff of sorts, where perching birds became the notes of some ephemeral fugue. And you don't have to believe him, but Colter said he could spend hours at his picture window, his jobless afternoons, with hands in pockets, looking through the plate glass at the score that his feathered friends composed on the wires (blackbirds for quarter notes and sparrows for quavers, I'd say), the melody line changing each time they took flight.

Lightly scratched by power lines hovering close to the roofs, the sky had all the room it needed to deploy over the low-slung bungalows that, once you looked closely, seemed to be huddling beneath it like frightened animals, vaguely aware of a danger they were unable to name.

But once named, the threat will often turn real.

The houses did well to keep their low profile with the overwhelming majority of sky bearing down on them. Colter's house in particular.

Because the truth is that the pastel roughcasting (Colter did mention the pastel roughcasting), the gleaming white garage door (I haven't spoken yet about the white garage door that glittered like a silver screen), the pediments I've already mentioned and the bow window with its flowered curtains that immediately caught the eye and had you imagining the cocoon inside, the wallpaper in saturated color that enclosed everything that Colter held dear, his wife and offspring who would rush to greet him when he arrived home from work (the daily odyssey, the return of the father and husband each evening), this house now belonged to the past.

The scene at the banker's, however, I mean the primal scene, by which I mean the afternoon when the banker approved the loan, telling him to sign here, and here, all kinds of forms where he had carefully written out his name, or his initials—he was told to initial the forms, as the term goes—doing as he was instructed to do, trying his best, looking at the financial advisor's fat finger (nail bitten to the quick, unsightly cuticles) that pointed to the places he needed to sign and initial, which Colter did, signing and initialing where indicated, and in doing so, he sweated, less because of the enormous sum of money at stake than because he feared making mistakes in the paperwork, because his signature was irregular, unsteady, requiring great concentration to make it look the same on every page: that afternoon was one of the most glorious afternoons of his life.

He pushed through the glass door and into the outside, strode down the avenue, buoyed by the feeling that he had just turned a page, as the saying goes, and he walked up to the threshold of this new chapter, luxurious and radiant, that was about to begin.

Betty's Heart

I BELIEVE IT can actually happen, that at the very moment you recall an intense happiness that later turned catastrophic, you can still experience the visceral sensation of that happiness, bizarre as that may seem. It's as if, by sheer concentration, you can relive the emotion despite the sorrow to follow. The powerfully happy memory of that glorious afternoon could still overwhelm Colter, even now.

That irretrievable feeling (or nearly impossible to retrieve, as when Phil was born, or when they brought little Betty home from the hospital, the sky studded with stars, glowing like embers, with Phil waiting at a neighbor's house, that pervasive, overpowering, supreme notion that, yes, he had finally made it), Colter could experience it yet again, like some grand illusion. It would come over him in a flash, a recovery of lost happiness rendered for only a few seconds, but so intensely, violently intact, as if the memory had remained in some pure state: Colter was able to artificially reconstitute the enchantment and relive the moment in all its raw intensity. But soon after came the pain, the notion of collapse.

It all started when there was no more work (the factory where Colter was working closed down fairly quickly) and he couldn't make the payments. At that point, things began to sour in the heart of Colter's wife.

Betty, no doubt about it, she had dreamt of something very different. Something other than absent paychecks and threats of eviction that grew more specific with each registered letter; she would throw out the notices without signing for the letters, hiding behind the flowered curtains whenever she saw the postman coming, or when she heard the sound of the brass knocker, which they hadn't installed so that someone would come knocking one day and wave an eviction notice in their face—officially stamped and awaiting their signature—signifying the prospect that everything behind that door, everything they normally called home, would soon no longer be theirs.

Nor was that knocker meant for the sheriff, who could also decide to stop by, with the hale, healthy looks and broad shoulders of one who appreciated law and order, with that compassionless expression of his, and something craven in those jowly cheeks, something lumbering and unbending about his entire body, both muscular and fleshy, a tall frame but with rolls of fat bulging here and there, stretching his cotton shirt. She couldn't face that, his dense hunk of a body and the unpleasant person inside, that narrow-minded, shrunken soul, unyielding as a bullet lodged in her heart when he would say You and your kids and your husband, you're going to have to pack up and vamoose out of here, him just standing there in front of her, and her not knowing what in the world to do, her life collapsing around her while he's standing there in her living room, his big body, and her body.

And she made a point of telling Colter, once the children were in bed, as she stood looking out the bow window with her back to him, watching the headlights of passing cars, that this wasn't the life she had hoped for, she, Colter's wife, standing straight and stiff in front of the window, rubbing her own shoulders as if she were taking herself into her arms. Streetlights splashed onto the moving vehicles, and in the glow, she could occasionally make out the silhouette of a driver—all those people who continued to come and go despite their tragedy, despite the specter of eviction that haunted their living room, and her world that was coming apart.

They were caught in the headlights of each passing car as they holed up in the shadows, she standing by the window and he sitting further back, unearthed momentarily by a flashing beam. A mobile beacon, like a rotating searchlight signaling danger, pulsating and insistent; and it seemed to be seeking them out in the darkness, abruptly flushing them out of their clandestine lair.

So one day, and this is what Colter wanted to tell, one day, he walked up the avenue toward the soon-to-be-impounded house that awaited him, with all the hope he had placed in it, its three pediments and bow window, that bow window he so valued for the way it expanded the house outward, and for the Christmas tree that could be seen from the street every year when Christmas time came, little lights blinking day and night like beating hearts, so that everyone passing by would know there's a family living there, with their tree with its string of tinsel winding through the branches like a snake (though who would dare to make that comparison?).

So there he was, walking up the avenue, with only a couple dollars balled up in the pocked soles of his shoes worn paper-thin, causing him to feel every bump in the blacktop below. But that day, when he sounded the knocker, that cold, squat object, curled up in his palm that struck it against the flat, brass surface, making the same heavy, dull sound it always did, that day, no one came to open.

He had to use his key; and he opened the door into the empty hallway, empty as the living room and bedrooms were, the bedroom where they once slept together, Betty and him, and the children's room, whose stuffed animals were all gone now.

How long will it take, asked Colter, raising a helpless, questioning finger into the bar's acrid air, for a man who came home like that to his house, a house that he had sweat blood for, where he'd settled his nearest and dearest, only to find it empty, deserted by the very ones he'd acquired it for, or rather, wanted to acquire, since just as he could no longer say *his* wife, he had never really been able to say *his* house, because of what he still owed the bank on the mortgage (so that, even when they were living there together, he never stopped worrying over whether he could say *his* house, and not the bank's house, a house he was purchasing square inch by square inch, of which he owned how much, he wondered, as his eyes scanned the empty living room that looked like some vast expanse, almost beyond his reach, half a hallway, at most); how long will it take for this man, so that this moment of his existence, the moment when he opened the door onto a house of empty rooms, will finally cease bleeding like an open sore, poisoning his life?

On that day, Colter sat right down on the living room carpet and suddenly sensed not only that he was mired in a daunting present, but he could also feel a wave coming from behind, sweeping him away, a wave of the past that flooded the present, as if the past, Colter realized, would always eventually catch up with you. And crushed by that wave, perhaps, he fell unconscious.

He woke up early morning, when the light outside came in search of him through the window, as if to tell him to get out of there, to get in his car and hit the road, to just drop it all and move on.

Moving On

So yes, move on, that's what he did, he got in his car and hit the road, no destination in mind, straight ahead, forking randomly whenever a choice arose, deciding as things came, no master plan, no itinerary, no north or south, on impulse alone, just to experience the flip side of his blues, the happy corollary to this dreadful solitude which was (when you think about it) the exercise of his freedom.

Next, after a few days on the road, Colter ended up at the Blueberry Inn, parking his car in the lot on the edge of the woods, near the solitary row of mailboxes belonging to who knew which faraway house.

He sat down at the bar and, checking for the few rumpled dollars still in his pocket, he ordered a beer which he drank, his eyes stumbling upon his reflection in the smooth surface of the mirror that ran all along the wall behind the bar. What he saw wasn't very encouraging.

It was Wendy who served him, with her austere face, like the cinderblock walls of the place, her forehead as white as the cloud-covered skies that stored up the coming rains.

They exchanged a few words, his shapeless and slow, hers quicker and more energetic, without knowing that, from that moment on, words like those are what they'd be trading by the crateful.

Later, a guy came in, looking like the filthy rich type, or rich enough anyway to offer to buy Colter's car for cash—Whose wheels are those, the gray crate parked outside?—for the price he was ready to settle for.

Colter's car was a station wagon with a metallic finish that used to shine in its younger days, when he would wash it on Sundays with a garden hose, since that's what he did back then, of course, sponging it first with sudsy water; it felt so good dipping the sponge into the soapy bucket, his arm slipped under the handle. And he'd pamper it, out there in front of the house he was still paying off in monthly installments at that point, his tongue out just a little, the way everyone does, curved a little to the right-hand corner of the mouth, the sign that he was totally engrossed in what he was doing.

And then, less and less—car washing, I mean—when he was unable to meet his payments and everything in his life veered off course, days out of work and the fear of losing everything, and the peculiar shame he felt whenever he talked to Betty. He didn't feel like dolling up his station wagon anymore, even just to pass the time, and like the picture of Dorian Gray, the car began to bear the stigmata of his interior life. Colter tried to put a brave face on it, keep up appearances by taking care of himself, more or less, but the station wagon became the outward expression (accumulated dust, mud stains) of the deterioration, the true wear and tear in the heart of its owner.

And now, on the day I'm referring to here, when Colter stepped up to the bar of the Blueberry Inn for the very first time, his car fenders caked in thick yellow mud from the road, but also from months of neglect, layer upon layer that he'd allowed to accumulate. Dust everywhere, even the windshield was veiled: the station wagon's idea of triumph was now a thing of the past.

With his last dollars going toward beers, and no idea how he'd even begin to pay for a place to sleep, this guy's offer was a lifesaver, and they shook hands to seal the deal, palm to palm, each with his lot of lifelines, fortune and love, do we really ever choose?

Colter heard the station wagon start up and didn't even turn to look out the window, not even a glance as he let his last earthly belonging drive out into the gathering darkness.

The Guy Who Was Reading the Story of the Lewis and Clark Expedition

THEY DID RENT rooms at the Blueberry, yes, Wendy replied, so Colter settled in, on the upper floor right above the restaurant, from where you could probably still hear the motors of passing cars, each of which reminded you, despite the current feeling of suspended reality, that the Blueberry, with its ill-defined forest on all sides, was not all the world had to offer.

So that's what Colter listened to, from inside his little room, the steady sound of diesel engines that filtered through the pines at the foot of the inn, those semis rolling in from parts unknown on their way to somewhere else, some of them heading toward the ocean, others into the foothills, some with plans, hope and purpose, others for the pleasure of eating up the miles and feeling the fine curve of the globe beneath their tires.

It wasn't long before Colter met up with—excuse me, but I'm going to interrupt here; I'm looking out my window, and here's this woman I've never seen on the beach before, performing her moves, all bundled up in a coat without a hood, the wind constantly blowing her hair into her face while she tries to reverse the effect by turning into the wind and walking backward a few steps, clearing her field of vision; but with the uneven sand and the storm conditions, she turns back around, regaining her footing, but her hair is back in her eyes again, so she repeats the maneuver, teetering like a drunkard as she zigzags across the beach, alternating two inconveniences, imbalance and blindness, looking like a bobbin unspooling, turning and turning, facing into the headwind, then whirling around again, hair whipping her eyes, obscuring her path, and the wind that seems to want her gone.

So, as I was saying, it wasn't long at the Blueberry before Colter met Harry Dean.

I don't know when it was that Harry Dean arrived at the farm, or whether it was the working outdoors or the solitude that he liked, since there was no one but the farmer and him (and later on, Perry, but I'll get to him in a minute) living there.

As for the farmer, Harry mentioned his existence two or three times, but we didn't know a whole lot about him. Except that he was the silent type, and that this suited Harry just fine. All he did was give Harry instruction as to what had to be done—and that was early on, since now Harry knows what to do, and doesn't even get that much anymore—and that's about the extent of his contact. Except when he would ask him to come out into the fields with him, and there they would be, just the two of them, focused on getting a job done, absorbed in their movement, without exchanging a word.

Most often, Harry worked alone. The skies were gray, but the pale light made the work easier. The days were matte and lusterless, and the thick cloud cover voided all shadow. You lived without that dark cutout of yourself that usually follows you around, or that you follow, depending on which way you're facing. So that when the sun finally did come out, Harry Dean was all surprised to see his shadow in the barnyard. Like seeing an old friend again, wasn't it? One you hadn't seen for weeks. I believe he enjoyed that familiar figure, the way it kept pace with his every move, flowing lightly, lithely, sliding effortlessly over any surface, his smooth and recognizable double that he was so glad to have back.

And then one day, there arrived at the farm where Harry Dean was living a new tenant (picture him in round, steel-rimmed eyeglasses, you get the look), in a beat-up used car whose dents and scratches said something about how many miles he had come.

It was an exceptionally sunny day, and Harry was busy in the barnyard sweeping the flagstones, while his shadow pretended to be doing the same, striving scrupulously to reproduce his every move, imitating him to the millionth of a second, a pointless circus pantomime that Harry allowed his grayscale cutout double to perform unhindered.

By way of luggage, Perry (that was his name), who had scarcely extracted himself from the vehicle than his shadow double was also cast onto the ground, had nothing with him but two books and a notebook.

The two books he'd brought along, I might as well reveal it now, told the story of the Lewis and Clark expedition.

Lewis and Clark, you've probably heard of them, were a couple of nutcases, that's the least we can say (but we're going to try and say more). Broadly speaking, Lewis and Clark set out with dozens of men at their command—it's 1804 here—because President Jefferson made them the following proposition: he said, Guys, how about traveling across America, east to west, and making note of everything you see along the way (and by everything, he meant tribes as well as flowers, terrain and fauna, the course of rivers, all the way to the Pacific, into which everything flows); this would be a huge step forward in our getting to know the territory. No problem, replied Lewis and Clark, and they chartered wagons and boats, and brought along gigantic notebooks where they would write everything down.

And that's what they did, wrote everything down.

The Lewis and Clark team took stock of the flora, bent their travel-weary bodies over plants, squatted and collected for their herbarium. They could be seen crouching over gentians and daisies, despite their attacks of lumbago; I say gentians and daisies, but there were also lupine and lily, and I also like the bear grass, with its big white panicles when it flowers. In the pockets of their military-issue jackets, they would collect umbellate pussy-paws, mountain heath and crowberry (plentiful in the region). And of course, *Mimulus lewisii.* I say of course because it is named after the explorer himself. Something about these Pacific-rim mountain flowers must have moved him, how quickly they wither. He must have knelt in the grass, his eye caught by a patch of these specimens: there was the flower, so defenseless, a gift, he stretched his hand out to the slender petals and held one between his thumb and index to gauge the texture (or the way they pinch the ear of a serviceman to say Good work, soldier, I'm proud of you). He pinched the ear of this flower and declared: I'm going to name you *Mimulus lewisii.* Of course, he said it in English, which came out as *Lewis Monkeyflower*, because something about it reminded him of a monkey, because he thought he saw, in the petals' design, the gaunt face of a baboon.

Lewis stood up; he was on a rise, not far from the ocean now, which he could almost feel, just beyond a patch of forest that lay between them and the water.

Getting back to the new farm tenant, he was originally from St. Louis, Missouri, which happens also to be the starting point of the Louis and Clark expedition. He got it into his head to follow in their footsteps, retracing their itinerary. Oh, not their literal footsteps—that would be asking a bit much—or even by canoe, as the expedition had done, alternating footpaths and waterways in rather precarious conditions, but in a used car that he had managed to buy with the earnings from his first desk job, where he saved up enough to afford this year of studious wandering. And the reason he stopped there in particular and lingered a while, at the farm where Harry Dean was living, was that the area where the Blueberry Inn was now located marked the approximate spot where the men of the Lewis and Clark expedition had to spend several weeks waiting out the rain that was preventing them from getting down to the ocean. And Perry, in an effort to reproduce this waiting period, drove the length and breadth of the farm in search of places where the men might have hunted, trapped, and dreamt of going home.

Motives for this kind of project are rarely pure. Perry had had a fiancée, Harry Dean was to find out later, a certain Mildred, who had left him, and this split most certainly had something to do with the trip, the decision to follow in the footsteps of Lewis and Clark, with a notebook to write everything down.

Field gave way to endless field under the vast, featureless sky. Sometimes, automatic sprinklers, slender and bristling like dinosaur skeletons (interminable spine sprouting ribs on either side), sprayed down on the crops seemingly by their own volition, though they were actually set in motion by who knew whom in the middle of these immense, uninhabited tracts of land. Further on, herds of bison would come into view, as Perry drove past (this was when he would drive near Tom and Lori Epler's ranch, for example, or around Brown's Buffalo Ranch, where Garret, Tim and Debbie Brown worked; there were Dan and Patty Armstrong, who also raised bison, Dan who fed the animals, and Patty, with her big glasses, more likely to be knitting or trying out new recipes, just go to her Facebook page and you'll see); and then, there was the fragmented forest broken up by clearings where clouds would cast oblong shadows that skimmed the crest of the grasses below.

While he was busy reenacting the expedition itinerary, stopping here and there to take stock and make note of the differences between the places Lewis and Clark experienced and today's landscape as seen from his car window, throughout this whole time, Perry must have been thinking, something inside him was rebuilding what Mildred had ravaged.

For Mildred's departure had left Perry in a state of stunned disbelief.

Over the weeks following their break-up, he would wake in the morning in his little apartment where she had so often spent the night, open the curtains on the unchanged street where everyone seemed to be going about their business, ignorant of what had befallen him. He would look out at the same pastel sky, tarnished by the car emissions rising all day from the passing traffic down below, surveying it all with the same composure, the same calm pallor it displayed back when Mildred was still around, when the two of them together used to open the curtain onto the city: and what struck Perry wasn't so much sadness as astonishment.

A sense of vague amazement that everything outside could go on without her (an irrational feeling that Perry struggled to overcome, but which kept reemerging, fueled by this lack of continuity between his own interior state (mortified, debilitated) and the world around him—vibrant, animated, alive) only compounded his bewilderment at Mildred's decision to leave. This unexplained departure that had left Perry flailing, for she was gone just like that, without a word. Yet, they used to talk together a lot back in the day, in parks, stretched out together on the cool grass, and at night as well, within the four walls of the bedroom; and then, suddenly, Mildred was onto something else, without even taking the time to explain, as if none of that had ever happened.

It was often in the evening, when Harry was out smoking on the stoop, and Perry was feeling idle after accomplishing the missions he'd assigned himself for the day, when darkness was falling, producing that unavoidable effect of the final curtain being lowered, when night obliterates day outright, finally and irrevocably, that's when Perry would be suddenly overwhelmed by Mildred's absence.

On the inside of the body, somewhere between sternum and stomach, something was hollowing out, and in that cavity, a sac was forming, tender and painful.

There were times (though rare, because of the thick layer of clouds, a regular feature of Oregon skies) when the stars would shine, and that was the worst, as if their twinkling were shooting a thousand arrows into that sensitive sac, intensifying the pain and sense of solitude. Maybe because the cloud cover always appeared so near (a low ceiling, familiar, almost reassuring), while the spikey shimmer of the stars reminded you of the infinite abyss of space, the vast distances between them and you, the sheer vertiginous immensity of it all.

The best thing Perry could do at that point was to go exchange a few words with Harry Dean. He would approach him, with Mildred still on his mind, torn between the need to bury that name somewhere deep inside, in an effort to drown the very thought of her, and the desire to talk about her, right there, right away, to Harry, to gorge himself on Mildred's name, which was all he had left, apart from the car he was traveling in and the two volumes to serve as his guide. They'd sit and talk a while, then Perry would go off to bed. Only later would Harry wander over to the *Ulysses*. Sometimes he wouldn't go at all, but would just sit and have a beer by himself, at his kitchen table, looking out onto the barnyard now cloaked in darkness, where the bright, geometric rectangle of Perry's window would project silently onto the graveled ground.

Haystack Rock

IN THE OFF-SEASON, said Tim (Tim Doyle, you know, the guy who runs the souvenir shop), every customer is like a survivor, to be treated with the respect due to those who have come out alive, and with the tiniest hint of suspicion as well. He wanders around the shop (testing a T-shirt, fingering a teacup, inspecting a figurine) and leaves with a bag of proof that he has been to Cannon Beach.

Every time the door chimes announce that a customer has stepped into the shop, it's an event. Tim sees the customer arriving, looking first at the window display from outside, bending over to examine a lamp or a bibelot: is he going to enter, he seems to be hesitating, then finally, yes, the stranger comes in to enjoy the warmth of the shop, they exchange a few words about the cold weather, and sometimes they'll start to chew the fat. But most of the time, visitors passing through the resort town in the off-season are loners, and it's up to you to invent what's going on in their heads, what kind of messy lives landed them here. And then, they're on their way, and you're none the wiser, you'll never know what melancholy thoughts they brought to stir up at this beach, in the hope that the sheer force of the wind and wildness of the waves would clear their minds.

Tim's display window features all kinds of figurines—noblemen bowing deeply from atop a stand, porcelain fish, if that's what you're into, wall plates, lamps studded with seashells (choose the one you like), a trivet with a blue and white sailboat motif, all items manufactured on the other side of the Pacific, but sold as local craft pieces with seashore, fishing and sailing themes. Inside, near the counter, what is especially eye-catching are the countless Haystack Rock magnets.

Because I actually haven't mentioned it yet, and you can't see from here, but it's an easy walk for anyone who wants to go have a look, you have Haystack Rock, outlined against the sky, all self-important, as if it knew that it serves as the emblem of Cannon Beach, giving its all to fulfill that function.

Let's use Haystack Rock as an excuse to play the tourist for a moment. It's one of the largest coastal sea stacks in the world, the locals will never fail to remind you. Picture a vast beach, nearly ten miles of sand, ocean, and sky (with seagulls where appropriate), and towering over it all, our timeless monolith, 235 feet in height, not exactly alone, but in dialogue with a series of rocky needles, dwarf sentinels placed as outposts. Inert and mineral, splendidly imperial, it confronts onlookers with a confounding geological enigma, almost makes their head spin when they start thinking of the ancient world it once belonged to, since we have such trouble even conceiving of such strange and powerful telluric phenomena, whose effects we can but contemplate, as we stand there with hands in pockets, staggered by the chasm of time separating us from some early seismic event and the energy that it must have involved.

All that business, in case you're interested, goes back some ten to fifteen million years. We're talking about the Miocene (not even a suggestion of Australopithecus yet, but plenty of seabirds already), volcanoes spewing like mad, and it is their lava flows, it would seem, that came to edify our monolith, the same way they formed many of the coastal features, eruption after eruption, until they created what's called an igneous province, a large territory composed of liquid lava that has cooled and finally congealed into this rock that provides the coastal cut we see today, with beaches here and there, picturesque agglomerations that, when seen set against the sky, give an impression of a tumultuous beauty.

Over time, the salt-laden winds and waves, if I've understood it right, have shaped and sculpted the rock mass into peaks and needles, and with regard to our Haystack Rock, into that broad, round form (because it's the sheer breadth of it that's so impressive), and must have brought to some folks' minds familiar rustic scenes (standing there on the shore, they must have recalled harvest time, mown hay pitchforked into piles on a hot, humid late summer day), so that they came up with the name Haystack.

But a haystack so huge that you're left with an impression of otherworldliness. Summer tourists may well sluggishly pile out their cars and drag their flip-flopped feet to the seafront, but when they lay their eyes on that, a wave of vertigo sweeps over them.

A chunk of basalt is what it really is (feldspar, olivine, clinopyroxene, and whatever else), and I referred to seagulls for convenience, but I should also mention the guillemots that nest up in their niches, the shiny brown cormorants that do their diving in the vicinity, the Bachman's oystercatchers with their long orangey-red beaks, walking the beach cautiously, and let's stop to observe the puffins swirling around it like black and white kites (depending on whether back or belly is exposed), endlessly restless silhouettes, and in stormy weather seeking refuge in the trough of the waves, strangely secure beneath the water's arc.

The members of the expedition must surely have seen those elegant, black-helmeted terns circling around the monolith, whose monumental proportions had the honor of striking Captain Clark's retinas (who blew his wad of adjectives to describe the rock: grandiose, imposing, magnificent, the most astounding landscape it had ever been his privilege to see);

and that's not including all the features not visible from here, like the anemones, the jumble of crabs, sea slugs, I could go on, that splash around in the tidal pools alongside limpets and chitons, all the little critters of the tidal range. For during this opportunity afforded by the ocean's retreat, the little tubs left behind are a-wriggle with starfish and their lascivious arm movements, hermit crabs poking their heads out of their borrowed shells to see what's going on in the world, gray shrimp sunning themselves in the calm puddles, a delightful change from the churning waves they normally have to cope with.

You're welcome to squat on the rocks and watch all these little swimmers (though multiple signs and tons of didactic handouts warn that you may not collect any specimens, ecosystem oblige) at low tide, when you can walk all the way out to the rock, so long as you time it right, be careful, and don't get caught out there when the tide comes back in: how many boats have they had to send out to rescue absentminded individuals stranded on the reef, how many times have they had to gas up the motorboats just to go save a careless visitor? And how often has an ill-advised off-season beachcomber got stranded out there and had to wait until the tide peaked and receded, clinging to the jagged surface, hands and feet lacerated by sharp barnacles, those crustaceans adhering to the rock so tightly and for so long that they become practically one with the rock, a good ten hours at the mercy of the wind, the sea's howl, the waves' crash, woe is us.

Picture a triangle, rounded at the top and anchored to a broad base, and that's Haystack Rock, bathed in every kind of weather, toughened by time, everlasting despite the relentless waves (a sight both reassuring and heartrending), proud and placid witness to the eons it has endured without a peep.

It must seem bewildering, wouldn't you think, to have been there for such a long time. It has watched all manner of hominids come and go, and then came the Indians, then the cowboys, then the men in cutaways, and now, in shorts and ball caps. And there it is, still showing its same stoically durable face—a benchmark.

Outside my windows, the rain has now completely evacuated the beach. My wind-whipped beachcomber has long since gone home, and now there's nothing but the timeless stretch of sand beneath the sky, with no marker as to what age this scene belongs to. Because one of the functions of these passersby is to timestamp the picture by their clothing, in the manner of carbon-14 dating. Deserted, the ancient, borderless beachscape is returned to itself, in all its raw, geological beauty, obeying a much slower and more comfortable temporality than the hectic, headlong, minuscule pace of a human life.

Lakeland

THE WAVE THAT crashed down on Colter, I'm back to Colter
now, when he entered that empty house, when he discovered,
one by one, the abandoned rooms, and even the stuffed animals
no longer enthroned on the beds (stuffed animals, he perhaps
had time to think, that the children went to the trouble to take
with them; as for their father, did they even say a word?), when,
in this kind of chaos (disaster), a house left behind by the very
ones who gave the place its meaning (and because Colter, you
can hardly blame him, had thought he'd finally made it, because
of that bricklayer's metaphor that everyone uses to talk about
relationships, and had wanted to "build" something with Betty,
without realizing that this dream is (sorry) the very denial of life
itself, which is mobile, fluid, ever-changing, requiring constant
vigilance, minute adjustments, trial and error, an ardent availability in the moment, don't you think?), when he went back
downstairs to the living room and fell to the carpeted floor,
sitting with his legs spread like a compass, his back against the
cold wall covered in the wallpaper he'd taken an entire weekend
to hang (Betty applied the paste while he managed as best he
could, fingers pinching the upper corners of each sheet, to carefully set it onto the wall, smoothing out any wrinkles with his
palm—a few times, looking like a real pro, he'd take out his
plumb line), this crashing wave, then, along with the thought
of losing Betty and the children, of their betrayal, along with the
prospect of their endless absence to come, it was like a return to
childhood. Like the feeling of an agonizing reenactment.

It was the memory of one winter's day, many years ago.

And that was another personal story Colter told us, later on, well after the one vaunting his bow windows, many evenings after describing the scene of the return to an empty house. He told this one only once, but how could I not remember it?

Picture a brick house heated by a single stove that was forever running out of wood. Two rooms: downstairs, a dining room separated from the kitchen by a hallway, and upstairs, Colter's parents' bedroom, where brown ceiling stains betrayed damp patches, despite the father's attempts at repair. When the rain was especially heavy, the water forced itself between the roof shingles and started pooling below, pressing on the plaster and slowly seeping in, forming droplets, two or three at first, that splashed noisily onto the floor, eventually gaining in number and speed, so that they rushed to place a bucket right underneath, cursing and swearing as they went, you make do with what you have. That's what the parents' room looked like, with its three or four assorted receptacles (salad bowls followed fast after buckets) placed wherever the ceiling was leaking. The downstairs room was just as bad. The walls were swollen with damp coming up from the ground this time, by capillary action (if you get my gist), since the house had no foundation.

The relentless rain, causing water to seep into the masonry from both top and bottom, combined with the inadequate heating, practically guaranteed that the house would smell sour and musty, which Colter would remember as the smell of childhood.

The child always slept in the hallway downstairs (what else can we do, the father would say whenever the mother expressed concern) on a folding cot that he would have to stow during the day.

Except that the day we're talking about here, he wasn't exactly a child anymore, but a sixteen-year-old, his mop of red hair

starting to veer toward brown (and is that the beginnings of a
beard I see, just a few stray hairs so far, widely spaced and in no
particular pattern), and his body already stocky and muscular.
He was working at an auto repair shop. I say repair shop, but
you have to picture a small courtyard with a toolshed where a
mess of tire irons, oil cans, bolts, and wrenches were scattered
around on old rags cut out of bedsheets. Who used to sleep in
these, Colter would often wonder as he cleaned some wrench;
and he would imagine cool rooms with shuttered windows
that opened in the morning onto a landscaped view; or night,
what, loneliness, pains reawakened, counting the strokes of the
clock; or the warmth of a body snuggled against you, you've
poured out your overflow. Sheets that had absorbed body fluids,
and ended up there, on those rickety shelves weighed down by
some filthy mechanic's tools lying around unimpressively in the
obscurity of the shed.

All of sixteen years old, Colter would continue wiping
his wrench while listening to some customer tell his tale of
tribulation. He knew that his job was all in the wrist (precise
yet unhurried, relaxed but not lazy, a sure thing, accomplished
with accuracy, though requiring no special concentration, since
habit takes over and gets it done), and in that special squint of
the eyes you had to learn to assume (which meant you were
listening with rapt attention, understanding, anticipating
what was needed to solve the problem at hand), and he would
punctuate the customer's litany of woes with knowing nods,
as if to acknowledge how much work it was going to take,
pretending to assess the magnitude, to pinpoint, to forecast, to
crunch the numbers, right, I think I got it, not a problem, but
it's going to take a little time.

A little time, which meant maximum dollars (scaling
proportionately for what maximum dollars actually represented
for someone like Colter, or even his boss), and it was the
customer's own fault for knowing nothing about car engines,

valves and other mushroom-shaped components, not to mention hoses, pistons, plugs (it took only a few words to convince him of your competence, like rods, cylinder heads or crankshafts—even pins and spindles sound impressive); the customer left with a package of beef jerky, which he gnawed on as he explored the vicinity on foot.

There was a lake not far from the auto repair shop, and on occasion, Colter would make a detour on his way home to go sit and look at the water, and the mirrored sky reflected back. The trees were upside-down, as with any lake, and didn't seem to mind that this was a manmade body of water.

Because, in a word, everything about Colter's childhood was on the shabby side, the cramped, damp housing, the auto shop that was nothing but a filthy little courtyard with a tool shack, and even the lake, dug out with a backhoe, plain and orthogonal, a fake lake, a pale imitation of what had given the burgeoning little town its name, Lakeland.

Lakeland: don't trust it, don't let that name set your imagination adrift. The place has nothing to do with a rolling green landscape, ready to shimmer each time a ray of sunshine pierces the cottony clouds, valleys filled with morning mists, nebulous enough to suggest a gentle mystery. No, not that at all. It just barely qualifies as a suburb, its streets laid out in an even grid, straight from the drafting table.

It was in this setting, neat and orderly, this townscape whose only ambition was to greet the passing day with an even distribution of tasks to perform, that Colter grew up, until the time came when all these straight lines broke into pieces, to form an inextricable tangle.

On the day in question, he was sixteen, as I said, he got home from work around five, and found his father standing in the doorway waiting for him; what's he doing there, Colter had the time to wonder, but he was also able to note something grim in his expression, pained and out of character. The father didn't beat around the bush; as soon as Colter had reached him, he said: your mother is dead. And it felt to Colter like the crossbeam of the doorframe they were standing under had just crashed down on his head. With just enough time for Colter to tell himself that no shock could be greater than this one. But it wasn't over yet.

The father had scarcely allowed a few seconds to pass, during which he saw the fear in Colter's face and glimpsed what was being taken away from the boy (his strength, his childhood, his mother's love for him, whose double-edged protectiveness disappeared along with her). He must have added that the firemen had removed the body, that there was no one in that room where Colter might be wanting to go, one foot already on the first step, and the father blocking his passage, because that's what the father did, he inserted his body between the first steps and the boy, an unwelcoming body, not one upon whose shoulder a child could cry for his dead mother, but rather, a rampart, a fence, the embodiment of thou shalt not. And not just because the mother wasn't in the room, not just because Colter had no more business in that part of the house.

It was because he had no more business in the house at all, he had nothing more to do with it.

Here is what the father explained to Colter, as he persisted in blocking his way to the staircase. He announced it in all bluntness, as if bluntly were the only way such news could have been announced, the only way it could come out, the words withheld all those years: he told him he wasn't his father. And that they no longer had any reason to be together under the same roof, now that she was gone.

I've packed your bag, said the father, in conclusion, the man he'd always assumed to be his father, with his imposing stature and serious, authoritative face (just the look you'd expect of a father in a little town like Lakeland), and who, in a few seconds, ceased to be. The bag was there in the hall, a gym bag, the biggest one he could find, midnight blue synthetic fabric (I don't actually know if it was midnight blue), with all the clothes he needed inside, a change of pants, sweaters, socks, briefs and a framed photograph of his mother—thoughtful of him, this father who wasn't his father, or was he just trying to get rid of the picture.

Colter leaned down to grab the bag, threw it over his shoulder and left.

He headed away from the house, down the interchangeable streets he'd so often walked along, lined with tight-lipped houses that must be harboring stories not unlike his own, stories of fathers who weren't the fathers. Some certainly had no idea, while others must have chafed as they waited for the day they'd disclose the truth (a sharp, caustic truth that would quickly dissolve all the ties that bind) to the uncertain offspring that had grown up without their asking to, and who these fathers who weren't the fathers, one fine day, finally managed to weed out.

Among those who had thus raised a stranger under their roof, one whose presence amounted to an insult to the ideal notion they'd had of their marriage, some could never bring themselves to tell the counterfeit children that they were fakes. These fathers would never be delivered of the stifling truth, hour after hour, meal after meal, as they playacted at being a family, plagued by the ever-present thought, even as the mother lifted the lid off the soup pot, that those same hands had done other things, must necessarily have performed other acts, for this other person at the table with them, the fruit of her womb, to look nothing like her husband. And those same husbands, in a surge of pride that did little to subdue the sting of jealousy, would infuse the atmosphere with their generosity of spirit, which they could bizarrely claim as a moment of personal glory, where they reigned supreme and magnanimous, knowing that, with one word, one phrase, they could upend this scene of uneasy peace; but they would swallow that word, that phrase, with their spoonful of soup in order to forge this fiction of harmony (their own creation, against all odds), which no one believed, in the end (neither the mother, naturally, who could sense, behind the fake father's every act of kindness, a resentment that spoiled each minute the three spent together; nor even the son, the pseudo-son who could feel it, without knowing the cause, who knew that this scene had somehow been miscast).

Anyway, Colter's sham dad was quick to remove the mask as soon as his wife was gone; and with the mask, the disguise they had foisted on the unknowing Colter since childhood, now so suddenly torn away, a costume that had dressed him up as the son of this man, so massive and austere. Colter, who was no longer the son, but only a fatherless teenager, and now mother-less as well, with nothing but a gym bag over his shoulder, just a boy about to leave the only town he had ever known, who had never seen anything but the brick houses of Lakeland and its manmade pond, who now had nothing to his name but a change of clothes, his freckles and his useless erections.

And Colter, walking by those houses full of their own suppressed secrets that could surface at any moment, walking with his minutes-old grief, his newfound knowledge, felt just then like a free electron, untethered from everything.

Laika the Dog

I WONDER HOW much time I spent sitting out in front of Moses's bar, in the thick, dark night, with only a rectangle of light from the window, casting a murky glow, barely lighting the street at all, matching the streetlamp's thin halo. I was letting the stories I'd just heard ferment in my mind, tales still smelling of the bar's steamy atmosphere, heavy with sweat and hops. You had to accept that these accounts were full of gaps, hazy areas, puzzle pieces that you'd attempt to fit together later on, bit by bit, until a picture started to take shape but would remain forever unfinished. Every night, I went home with a few more pieces of the puzzle that would pile up in my beer-addled brain.

Once Moses had closed up the bar, and Harry Dean, unfit to drive, would head home to sleep at Shannon's (arm in arm, they'd stumble into the night, riveted to each other, looking like some kind of four-legged crab reeling down the empty streets), it would sometimes happen that Colter, rather than joining his buddies' conga line, would sit down with me on the front stoop, right on the wooden step, and we'd feel the wind on our sweaty red faces, resting our arms across our knees.

I watched the smoke rising from my cigarette and blowing inland, twirling in the cold air, at first a concentrated spiral, then disappearing into nothingness as the wind whisked it away; and it crossed my mind, however confusedly (so small a thing we are) that everything goes up in smoke, which necessarily has to do with our memories, with the passage of time.

The street was quiet, I don't know what the dogs were up to, whether they were asleep in their doghouses. Anyway, it wasn't our shouting that was going to stir them, since we weren't saying a word, Colter and me. We were just sitting out there in the cool of the night, each to his own thoughts, and me smoking, because it was as if by breathing in, inhaling the smoke, you could hold in everything that was fleeing; don't know if you've had that feeling too, like taking it back in, ingesting it, gathering it all back together. And then when you finally exhale, expelling all that ephemera, even though you're letting it go, you at least get the feeling you've really enjoyed it.

One time, we actually did exchange a few words, Colter and me, and I guess you could say that things got a little heated.

The moon was fat and full that night.

Moonless nights, there were plenty of those as we would be leaving the bar, knowing that moon was up there somewhere behind the clouds, too shy, a no-show yet again. But for once, on the night I'm talking about, you could see it distinctly above the rooftops, with its light and dark patches (seas, for a long time, they were thought to be actual seas) and the moonscape of popular imagination, with its dusty valleys, chalky soil, and crusty craters.

When atmospheric conditions were just right, this is the first thing I thought of, the Lewis and Clark men would be sitting outdoors at night, looking through their telescope, treating themselves to a little stargazing on one of those rare clear nights, because that's the way they were, not ones to walk away from such a sublime moment, especially a scientifically motivated one. They shouted out the names of the constellations, making guesses, staring into the magnificent blackness, while, in their enthusiasm, they couldn't help experiencing fear at the idea of the great unknown looking down upon them.

What's for sure is that on nights when they slept out under

the sky, gazing up at the moon, with its changing phases, the milky disk that would shrink down ever thinner to a sliver and disappear altogether before swelling back into its signature fullness, it must have occurred to them that the very notion of setting foot on that surface was but the stuff of dreams. And here's where they would fall into that state of wonder we sometimes experience, as we tip back our heads and stare out into deep space, and feel as if we could tumble into an immense black hole.

The moon I see through my front window, on nights when sleep won't come, when the cloud mass thins away, allowing the bright disk to mirror into the dark ocean, a white pancake floating unmoored, is not quite the same one, a pure heavenly body, distant and untouched, that those men saw as they lay under their damp covers, heads resting on their rucksacks, eyes open onto the impossible, but a moon that has now known the footsteps of Man, and we might well think, from time to time, of the little flag that's planted up there now, waving at no one, in the absence of wind, solitary and pointless.

That's what it was, that night, that Colter was thinking about, as he stared at the full moon, fresh and white, he thought of those three guys who'd made it all the way up there, those puffy astronaut suits making their movements so ungainly, the lumbering, slow-motion strides of that one small step for a man (remember, that crackly voice coming from so far away), the footprint left on the powdery lunar surface when they planted the American flag in the pale flesh of the empty planet.

Because conquest didn't end when the settlers reached the Pacific Ocean, not by a long shot, for after the great westward push, they looked heavenward and wondered what might be up there to discover: generation upon generation, from blueprints drawn to bolts tightened into place, from raw smarts to sheer daring, Colter laid it all out for me, from skill to will, our space cowboys finally made it up there, and as if to prove that they had, for any hypothetical lunar inhabitants who would come inspect the strange object, with the same perplexity and wonder as had the Native Americans upon seeing the first tall ships approaching their shores, they raised the banner of their absurd victory, the shaft pounded deep into the lunar soil, a stake driven into the pale, ashy ground that it was.

Who knows how folks get ideas into their heads, but Colter got it into his that he could actually see it, that proud and solitary flag they'd left behind up there.

Our man seemed to scan the bright surface with laser-like precision, conceding that, yes, at such a distance, it's bound to be tiny, but that if you try hard enough, Colter mumbled on insistently, wait, look right there, and he pointed a finger at the big white ball, at some figment of his imagination that his eyes thought they were seeing.

Since I persisted in not making out anything (or, as Colter claimed, didn't want to make out anything, because that's what he figured, in the end, that I was refusing to see what was there, even as he directed his piercing gaze at that impossibly tiny dark dot against the milky white, what he took to be the flag), Colter concluded that I was simply unwilling to admit it, and here the taunting kicked in, it's because it'd make you feel lousy, wouldn't it, he declared, to admit that it's really up there, the patriotic banner waving in triumph against the lunar sky, that would make you feel like crap, you little cheese-eating surrender monkey, he said, basically, with his made-in-USA idioms.

We got up to leave, and the dogs began barking.

Every time we walked past the fence, they would howl into the dark night, the ones that weren't allowed to sleep inside, and who hung out in the yard while their master was asleep.

Those hounds would pace up and down that fence in an endless loop of solitude, locked in under leaden skies, and wouldn't the arrival on the scene of a few wasted clowns like us come as an unhoped-for distraction? You'd have thought that three boozers out there in the middle of the night would have provided the dogs a welcome relief from (what I imagine were) their bitter ruminations over the canine condition, that they would have gladly allowed us to climb over the fence and crash on the lawn, or, catching sight of the begonias (as if the prospect of begonias had at last given meaning to our mission, something to strive for with all our unsteady strength, eyes fixed on the tiny petals, tarnished by the lack of light), relieve our beer-filled bladders (since urinating on flowerbeds is something that a dog-mind could comprehend); the dogs could have entertained themselves by snapping at our pant legs, or unearthing an old plastic bone and coaxing us to play fetch, where no matter how many times you threw the damn thing, the damn dog would chase and return, his night vigil having suddenly turned into a carnival.

But there's worse than boredom to overcome. There is the thought of their master asleep behind the façade, and their desire for his acknowledgement, since every moment of a dog's life is invested in this aim to please, to receive whatever tokens of gratitude the master thinks his pet deserves. Which is why they dig deep into their voice box to produce the widest range of sounds—listen to how these low and high barks alternate to create a strange, undulating pattern—discouraging any potential trespasser. That's why dogs bark, and that's why they were barking that night when Colter and I were passing by, out of some obscure, hard-to-fathom affection for their masters, who don't allow them onto their beds, or on the carpet, or even in a cushioned doggie bed set up for them in the hallway, but leave them to sleep outdoors in the rough, waiting expectantly for day to dawn, when they might earn a flattering word, a pat on the head that will make them feel needed.

That night, walking back to the motel after leaving Colter in front of Shannon's apartment, I started thinking about the dog they sent into space before the first manned flights. It was the first time a living creature had been put into orbit. The Russians had chosen what looked to me like a female German shepherd, but it was actually some cross between a terrier and a husky, as far as anyone could tell, and answered to the name Laika. I once saw a photo of her: from profile, lying on her side, body bristling with electrodes, mouth open, eyes looking straight ahead, doing her best to do as she was told, not suspecting for a moment that the people fussing around her, whose orders she was so submissively obeying, with all the affection she could muster, were in the process of contriving a little space mission for her, just to see how her organism would behave, since they all had big plans to make it someday to the moon, whose white form the dog must certainly have seen from down in the streets of Moscow, where the winter sun sets so early, walking on his leash like so many other dogs, moving cautiously along the snowy sidewalk among the urban throng as it went about its earthly business. And I wondered what she experienced, all alone in her little spaceship, whether there were windows, whether she could see into bottomless space where the spaceship was headed, what images were going through her doggie mind as the trusting creature was suddenly plunged into interstellar solitude.

The Three Volcanoes (An Indian legend)

EVERY TIME HARRY would come by the Blueberry in the evening to pick up Colter and drive him to Moses's bar, he retraced the itinerary of the Lewis and Clark expedition. And soon, the stretch of slate-gray water would come into view through the foliage, the endpoint that the explorers had so long aspired to see, and which our two oddballs reached in a half hour, on a blacktopped road that their pickup absorbed as cleanly as a retractable tape measure. And I say the slate-gray stretch of water only for the seasons when there was still daylight at that hour, because in the winter, all you had to go by was the sound, so unmistakable, when you'd open the vehicle door, the sound of folding waves, of water being sucked back and flung forward, alternating rumble and slam. That, together with the salty air, in case you weren't sure, when you got out of the truck, since you were in the total darkness, that you were actually on the ocean front, that whiff of iodine, that gust of wind that swirled around the houses at the first opportunity, channeled by their facades.

Harry and Colter would then walk the few steps separating them from the *Ulysses Returns* with the ocean at their backs, that noisy, mind-bending, and omnipresent mass that continued to shine at the end of the grid-like streets we sometimes crossed.

Ever since Harry began to talk about them, the image of the Lewis and Clark expedition team would waft around the bar, in between the beer mugs, the silhouette of their loose overcoats, weary specters gliding among us in the moist air, seeking a little warmth, and I could picture them hiking along the trails, eyes

on their feet so as to avoid slipping on a wet rock and falling
under the considerable weight of their packs, and the rains, I
picture how it must have poured, like a shower of spears, pounding down on their bodies, how they were pummeled by the clue-
less sky like a gang of convicts marching to the whip, the same
rains they watched from inside their makeshift shelters, the same
endless supply of water that leached the land and the mind.

And that's how it was, after countless months of rough
journeying, there they were, so close to the end, stuck for weeks
by the rains, only thirty miles from the ocean.

Clark sometimes went ahead to scout.

One day, we find him climbing up a 200-foot cliff and he
spots a snow-peaked mountain in the distance. Shielding his
eyes with his hand, he observes the form and concludes that
it is Mount St. Helens, just as Vancouver had described it.
Historians now believe, however, that it must have been Mount
St. Adams, since Mount St. Helens, it seems, is not visible from
what was Clark's vantage point.

St. Helens or St. Adams, either way, it's volcanoes we're
talking about.

And that's what I'm getting at here. Because I haven't really
said anything about volcanoes, except to talk briefly about how
the rock on Cannon Beach was formed (the igneous province,
remember, forged out of lava), but volcanoes do weigh a little
on the region, in a rather discrete way, which is what makes
them sneaky.

To put it plainly, these volcanoes are not always aboveboard.

Not the kind of volcanoes that emit smoke day and night,
that rise up threateningly out of the landscape like some kind
of sinister reminder that we're all mere mortals; nothing to do
with those hostile, dramatic silhouettes that strike terror in our
hearts, filling the sky with their plumes and our souls with a
sense of our own precariousness.

These two look so downright friendly that everyone has got used to taking hikes around them on Sundays.

So, Mount St. Adams. It's probably been ten centuries since anyone took notice. You'd swear it was just another peaceful mountain, a pretty easy climb, too, involving no major technical difficulties. You should probably watch out for coyotes and bears, Harry warned, if you're planning to camp under the stars (though he must have figured I wasn't the type to go sleeping on a bed of pine needles in the dark with danger lurking all around).

Mount Hood (which I haven't mentioned yet, but there's also Mount Hood), from what I've understood, is still active, but the last time it let go with an eruption dates all the way back to the eighteenth century. Since then, people have been setting up their tents carefree, slipping into their sleeping bags and falling asleep, dreaming of the fried bread breakfast they'll be making on their camp stove the next dew-soaked morning. A cushy, easy-does-it, welcoming kind of volcano, in a word, one you have to beg from time to time to exhale a few photogenic plumes into the sky that will quickly dissolve, just long enough to inspire caution and respect with this harmlessly intimidating effect that we all adore. And then it returns to its baseline apathy, its lazy, unmovable pose, a vague kindliness emanating from its inert, stable mass.

With Mount St. Helens, though, things get more complicated.

Like the others, it has built a relationship of trust and familiarity with the inhabitants. Here too, folks are accustomed to heading out there to stretch their legs on the weekend. Its periods of dormancy lasted centuries, and no one saw any reason for concern as they hiked up its trails, picnic basket in tow, picking the occasional woodland strawberry or, yum, a tangy wild blueberry.

And then, that confidence, a short while back, Mount St.

Helens betrayed it.

It was one day in 1980, in the spring, I believe. A day that no one around here feels much like talking about.

Nineteen-eighty, I looked up at Moses and back at the picture, and tried to do the math: how old would he have been then? Same age as the boy in the picture? It occurred to me that this might have been it, the frightened smile, the memory of the eruption, something he saw, something that happened to someone he knew.

I would have to be able to read Moses's mind, but no one here could do that, least of all me. The night Harry was talking about Mount St. Helens, he continued wiping his beer mugs clean as if none of that had anything to do with him.

Yep, Harry continued, but there's also that story they tell about the three mountains. Because the Indians, back when they could sit long evenings unmolested under the stars around their campfire, they wove a legend (everyone brought something to the table, so that they ended up not knowing who had said what, and the story became a single creature all its own, expanding a little every night) to explain the origin of the three peaks.

Here is the legend, which I in turn will now tell.

The three mountains, believe it or not, had not always been mountains.

There was a time long ago when they were flesh-and-blood creatures. Here's what happened.

An Indian god and his two sons were roaming the country. It was a pleasant, manly journey among kin. They would gallop into the wind, clouds high in the sky (oh, the feeling of one's body engaged in that rustling mass of moving air), and slow to a trot, conversing, all the while sensing bittersweetly that this first outing together would also be their last. Each of the two sons would go on to live his life, as sons always do, and this was good, thought the father, for this was the way of the world. He only wanted to communicate to them a few necessary truths, that they might become brave and gentle. These delicate words fluttered around them like multicolored butterflies.

Yes, but here's the thing: a father's wisdom does not preserve you from all harm, and the sons' apprenticeship was far from over when their path crossed that of a beautiful girl upon whom both boys, as if by some evil coincidence, set their sights.

The situation was rendered all the more inextricable in that the girl seemed unable to choose between them. This double homage rendered her by two sons of a god, no less, must have gone to her head. Giving each the fullest consideration (alright, let's focus here, she said to herself), it seemed to her that each had appreciable qualities. But also, let's face it, a few shortcomings as well, both of them, though upon close inspection, they were not the same for each. So, which list of flaws was worse than the other? Which list of qualities clearly superior? It was so hard to decide, and the girl started whimpering, unable to come down on one side or the other.

Her hesitation was quick to irritate the two sons (put yourself in their shoes), driving them mad with anger and desire.

They saw no other solution than to battle each other for the prize.

In this regard, at least, they were in agreement: they would do it without telling their father, who was likely to frown upon the project—and whoever won would get the girl.

Let's not forget, however, that these two vainglorious, lovesick brothers were of divine origin: this was no trivial duel. Each mustered the means at his disposal. Pyrotechnics as only gods can produce, tree trunks ripped out of the ground and launched like mere javelins, encampments razed in one sweep because they happened to be in the way, thunderbolts brandished like daggers, entire forests burnt to the ground, scenes of devastation throughout the country.

Upon discovery that his sons had laid waste to the land, the father flew into a rage (I mean, would you look at this mess, uprooted pines every which way, and couldn't you have been a little more careful with the teepees where actual people are living, Lord almighty, what did I do to deserve kids like this), and brought the havoc to a halt by means of a draconian punishment: having no qualms (or did he? Doesn't a father's heart ever feel doubt?), he turned his sons into mountains (today's Mount Adams and Mount Hood). And while he was at it, ditto for the conflicted damsel (today's Mount St. Helens), without whom, you have to concede, none of this would ever have happened.

Mary's Fringed Skirt, the Doberman and Two or Three Little Things I Need to Explain

SURE, I COULD have chipped my two cents' worth into the common pool of stories told at Moses's place. Not sure what kept me from doing so.

Would things have turned out different if I had spoken, if I had told them things? Is there any way of ever knowing? I don't have an answer for that.

One day, Shannon asked Moses something having to do with the name of his bar, he wanted to know whether this Ulysses guy ever did make it home, in the end.

Nobody there had actually read the epic, I don't think, but they'd heard of some episodes, not sure how, maybe from movies, or from a children's book of legends, a Christmas present from some aunt (one of two or three books in the entire house, the second of which was a cookbook, the other an atlas of some sort where they'd stare at the outlines of countries they'd never get to visit, tinted inexplicably in pink, orange or purple, with only the blue of the ocean connecting you to something recognizable and real), an abridged version of the original that this father or that mother might have read aloud to them, at bedtime, though they more likely fell asleep all on their own. (Colter's mother propped up on the cot in the hallway, book in one hand, and the fake father stewing in the bedroom overhead, waiting for her to come upstairs, at which point she'd get the same lecture on how long it had taken her, why does it take you so long, Christ, with his desire mounting under his striped pajamas, growing painfully difficult to contain.) The mother, by reading these bedtime stories, tripping over the syllables, labored to make reparations for the lie she was compelled to tell her son with regard to the real father, and the deep separateness this knowledge created between them, despite her love for him, or maybe some teacher told the legend of the famous odyssey, glorifying the challenges and obstacles, how huge the whole journey was, while the kids imagined a bearded adventurer in a rocky terrain, who always managed to come out on top, the kids who, for once, were really listening, more interested in the action scenes than in the wife who would weave at her loom to pass the time, awaiting his return, who were more concerned with fighting monsters, throwing spears and waging hand-to-hand combat on the burning sands.

With his ship stuck in the doldrums, Ulysses pacing on deck, cooling his heels, the sea like a mirror, the ship's sails inert, not even a breeze. Either that, or a shipwreck, hull split in two, barely enough time to dive into the drink and swim ashore, and now what do we do? Living the MacGyver life, rafts to be built, and there you are, sailing once again, treacherous shoals to navigate, monsters to slay, sirens to embrace, Ulysses was no slacker, why so long to get home, then, forever delayed by a hitch or a snag. Barely escaping from one impossibly tight spot than our Mr. U falls right into another. And every time, he and his men set sail again, plowing the unfaithful waves, and always something, every time, something that delayed the moment he would set foot on his island.

It was Harry who spoke up, answering yes, Ulysses did make it home by the end of the story. Colter and Shannon felt relieved at first by the idea of return (is relieved the right word here?), but Harry Dean added that what happened next wasn't such a pretty picture. The return of Ulysses was a bloody one. It was Harry who said that the story ended in a bloodbath. At least, that's how he thought he remembered it, ending in a massacre.

And it was that final scene then, naturally, that hung in the air within the wooden confines of Moses's bar, where the moist, malted air had a way of jinxing everything.

Whenever I dig further into the matter, when I turn things over like clayey earth, heavy and clinging, I can't help wondering whether some plot was being hatched from the very start, and is plot-hatching really the right word, or was it just rotten luck, in the wrong place at the wrong time, who's to know? Because here's the thing that's been gnawing at me: in this whole story, I never once thought I'd turn out to be the hero (victim, too, but also the hero, in a way); or did I know, did I secretly suspect that this would happen, and did I just let it come to pass, jumping feetfirst into the lion's maw? Or even worse, an awful assumption, maybe I wished it to happen, a notion that streaks across the skies of my mind like a raven, a sniggering silhouette I'm quick to chase away. What is my share of guilt in this business, how innocent am I? When I think about it, I sometimes feel like there were two of me, the one who suspected and the one who turned a blind eye.

I've got the notion that the whole thing is the ocean's fault.

Something about the lay of the land, how battered and broken it is, worn away by salt and squalls until it crumbles; and trees, turned all inside-out, twisted branches, buffeted and deformed, playing opposite the giant boulders, all of it reeking of rage and decline. Everything about it is stubborn, perpetual, insoluble; it must have been eating at them, Colter and the others, stirring up a kind of blind resentment.

The ocean, it's not so much that they were thinking about it all the time, but still, there was no getting away from it. There was something unsurpassable about it, this heady country of theirs that they all came to resemble.

And the more they heard the ocean crashing onto the

shore, heaving and headstrong (chipping away, eroding, its salty venom seeping into everything), vindictive, foaming with unfathomable rage; the more the ocean imposed the spectacle of its unfounded anger, a wrath immemorial that fed upon itself, pounded the shore with immeasurable energy, the same unrelenting fury, the same splendidly unmotivated restlessness, the more they resembled it.

And they were all of that, I thought, both the fragile sand that the ocean so relentlessly bludgeoned (weren't their past wounds inflicted in the manner of surf on a beach, the docile, submissive, passive beach that takes it without flinching, a bit more damaged with each blow?), and the roiling water, capable in turn of inflicting great torment.

At Moses's place, it was Colter who opened up most often, that's a fact. And when he wasn't saying much of anything, just sitting there scowling, his torso stooped over his beer, his thorax a crypt, and in its hollow, the beer mug glowing like a candle, this is what he must have been brooding over, the broken windows of his house open onto the deserted street, the wind sweeping in and shredding the curtains into streamers. A bleakly festive setting, where perhaps new occupants, scrawny, anxious squatters sitting on the moldy, rain-soaked carpet, whose tired bodies and worried thoughts had taken possession of the premises that had once contained his cozy family story.

Harry Dean, with his tall, lean frame, String-Bean Harry (or asparagus spear, or some other skinny vegetable they'd call him, just to jibe, because even as thick as they were, the trio did have their tense moments, this three-pack they formed at Moses's place), would gladly talk your head off, but as you've seen, it was always about Perry, or the farm, or the Lewis and Clark explorers, the local volcanoes and their legends: about his own life, not a word.

What about Shannon? He could be coaxed to talk, less often

than Colter, but there were things he did say.

They came out little by little, at least when I was there, and before he got to the really dark stuff, which didn't surface until much later, there were little hints, leads, that would help you understand him.

First of all, when Harry Dean seemed fine with his bachelor's life, Shannon would say that sometimes freedom comes at a cost, that sometimes the price is too high. He would just toss that out into the stale air of the bar, a statement that would resonate in mysterious waves, both alarming and pedagogical, as if to say, heed my words.

And whenever Colter talked about the empty house, about Betty taking off, Shannon would have this to say about his own case (when the baton of confidences, as it were, was passed to him), about the house he too had bought (for Shannon also had himself a little house with his little family inside), but had left, we were to learn, because there was no place for him there, or because he had the feeling there was no place (he'd get home in the evening, a fly in the ointment is what he felt like, with the children bawling, unaffectionate toward him, and his wife, once she had fed the children and put them to bed, would refuse to give herself to him), and this is what Shannon would say, that a man who leaves his house, with his children and their mother inside, is a man in exile.

Sure (Shannon would add), there was Mary, his new homeland, there was the little apartment with Mary (and also, at first, the Doberman, I haven't said anything about the Doberman yet); but that was Shannon's point, that exile, even if you're the one who chose it, is still exile. That you enjoy everything that's new and so much better in the new host country, but that you still carry with you an inexplicable, almost poignant regret.

A weird nostalgia, Shannon concluded, for a world you're unlikely to ever return to, but where you've left behind something of yourself.

I'm not sure I should be talking about the Doberman, or if it would be helpful for you to know that Shannon named his Doberman Joe, after a cousin by that name who was very close to him when they were kids. The cousin must have had something in common with the dog (what, I don't know: facial expression, a shifting light in the eyes, the way he held himself?), though Shannon hadn't heard from him in years. But all he had to do was to call Joe, to pronounce the name, for the faithful Doberman to arrive at the scene, ready for any situation, obedient and efficient.

He would talk about the Doberman on occasion over at the *Ulysses*, but in a way that made us wonder what all this cousin business meant, since he'd told us practically nothing; still, we sensed there had been a disappointment, and also that childhood thing that sometimes came back and seemed to anchor everything else in life, the breeding ground of childhood mostly gone and forgotten, a version of one's self that is unfinished and unstable. And so dependent on others.

We never found out how the Doberman died, but in the early days, Mary had accepted it into the little apartment (despite all the drooling and the not exactly friendly-looking fangs, the muscle-bound body of a dog that eyed Mary as one that knew it outweighed her, while it gazed at Shannon as if to say you are my world) (the Doberman that would spend the evening scratching at the door whenever Shannon spent evenings at the bar, anxiously awaiting his return), just as she accepted that Colter and Harry would sometimes crash on the foldout bed in her living room when they were in no condition to drive the pickup back to the Blueberry and out to the farm.

Sitting on the stoop in front of the *Ulysses* once they had left, I imagined them fully clothed and sprawled out on the pull-out couch-bed, open but unmade, snoring away in the living room, on the other side of the wall from where Shannon and Mary slept. Shannon would also be sleeping like a log, as you might figure. She must have lain there listening to them all snoring, their stale beer breath filling the air, their bodies sunk deep into their mattresses. And in the oceanic night, Mary (this is what I thought to myself) felt strangely protected by the snoring males around her, by this noisy breathing, uninhibited, serene and primitive.

Mary, with her fringed skirts, if you're interested, Mary, if you'd like to hear more about her, with those fringes that fluttered when she walked.

Mary never went to the *Ulysses*, but you could see her during the day, in the streets of Cannon Beach, on her way to the grocery store where she worked part-time, or just out for a walk, often with Shannon at her side, he who always had some comment to make about the way she dressed; it was just like Shannon to start in with the insults, to speak out whenever the slightest thing vexed him. But she just bounced along the sidewalk and ignored him, acting like she didn't give a damn about Shannon's moods, seeming to all the world unsinkable, even though she was anything but, inside (Mary's life was a frail skiff), where she kept her fragility a secret, concealed under a smooth surface of kindness and goodwill. That was Mary.

Mary, with her fringed skirt (will you stop wearing that skirt, Shannon would say), Mary with the fringes that sway with her hips, and Shannon trailing behind her, ranting about how all of Cannon Beach can watch the fringes swing with Mary's every step, every joyous, carefree stride, as if it were the skirt itself (or the simple joy of wearing it) that made her gait so bouncy and nimble. That's when Shannon's laugh would sound phony, more high-pitched than usual, sharper than when he laughed wholeheartedly (assuming he was ever capable of an honest, full-spirited belly-laugh), and because there's sometimes something untamed about laughter, about the sudden emotion that triggers the noisy release, as if self-propelled, taking even the laugher by surprise.

Shannon's laugh would come out in stupid, jealous bursts that would follow in Mary's wake like a swarm of flies, or better, mosquitos, wasps, a cloud of noisy and possibly evil insects. That's what Shannon's laugh was like, the notes of his laugh, in such situations.

Mary dealt with it the way she did with everything else in her life. Things seemed to just slide off her as she made an effort to find something positive, no matter the circumstance, something good in even the very worst situation; that was Mary's theory: you'll find that joy is always possible, if you pay attention.

Still, those fringes had a way of tickling the backs of Mary's knees as she walked, Shannon watching like a hawk, and the wind also played tricks with the fringe's ripple, all the while forcing the clouds overhead to scud by, dragging all that vaporous mass across the sky, constantly rearranging the contours of the heavens, so mobile and voluminous, yet blowing so softly against Mary's legs.

As I sat there on the stoop outside the bar, I tried not to think too hard about the fringes of Mary's skirt. The same wind that was on such friendly terms with that fringe during the daylight hours as it swept through the streets of the town, I let that same wind sober me up. I looked at the darkened facades splattered here and there by the light from streetlamps, and could feel two, three thoughts taking shape again.

In the distance, the volcano wasn't breathing a word.

Johnston, Blackburn and the Rest

HERE'S WHAT REALLY happened that day in 1980, what no one really wants to talk about.

You first have to know that there had been small quakes during the previous two months that should have sounded the alarm. Observers had been crisscrossing the area in jeeps, doing the math, making their tentative forecasts, but opinions diverged. There was one voice, however, that of David A. Johnston, a volcanologist, to warn that the situation was serious. But most others downplayed the danger. They basically called for calm, explaining that these were common volcanic phenomena: another couple of tiny shocks, and everything will fall back into place.

Johnston kept insisting that just the opposite was true. And in fact, magma was upwelling and seeping into the mountain, causing distortions, outcrops, fissures, and cracks.

The battered mountain shook beneath the impassive sky, flanks quaking, as magnitudes were recorded, still no cause for alarm, they said.

On some days, they registered up to one hundred quakes. The specialists (apart from Johnston, of course, everyone but Johnston) were categorical: there was no risk of eruption. Except that we ask you to avoid hiking in snowy areas, because of the heightened risk of avalanche, if you'd be so kind.

Temporarily, folks found other ways to spend their weekends.

No risk of eruption, you said? Mount St. Helens made liars out of the experts. Like it'd had enough of being condescended to, of everyone minimizing what was going on under there.

For starters, we'll give them a few phreatic eruptions. Here we go, vroom! Explosions of water and steam, there goes one hell of a plume for you, billowy white, but gray ones too, full of ash and even bits of rock.

Oh, so they want more, do they? Fractures, and eventually the formation of a second crater, which is hardly a good sign— but still, the scientists dig in their heels.

How much more do you need, lightning, maybe? Thunderclaps, an electric storm slicing the sky in half with an earsplitting crack?

The scientists have seen worse than this, but the local officials declare a state of emergency. People who live around there (especially the owners of resort restaurants) are evacuated. Down below, there are the inevitable rubberneckers who turn out to watch the show. And the mountain gives them their money's worth: an enormous bulge starts to form, expand, and move. The mountain is swelling, and the Helens bruise is looking like really bad news for everybody.

Johnston is there, keeping watch, weighing his options. He has been spending entire days sitting in his canvas chair next to his RV, watching the summit through binoculars, jotting down observations in a notebook. He occasionally leans back onto the white corrugated aluminum siding of his camper, feeling the warm undulation against his back.

David A. Johnston, I haven't properly introduced him yet: thirtyish, born in Chicago, had been around quite a bit, Alaska, Colorado, Michigan, and always for his training in volcanology.

What does it feel like, to be watching for a volcanic eruption? One little man there on the scene, with all of his expertise, his stats, as he faces down the monster in this strange and unequal arm-wrestling match: what game is he playing here? He who, unlike his colleagues, really believes an eruption possible, he who is so vigilant when it comes to safety and prevention, what was he doing out there, so near the crater, in his striped canvas folding chair?

The slopes are still trembling and, look closely, the summit has taken a hit. It's losing its classic profile as it morphs into an approximation of itself. There's no denying it now, it's starting to collapse. And there's that bulge, that damn bulge, says Fred (at quite a distance from there, hunched over computers behind a plate-glass window, completely out of range), scratching his head, and at the US Geological Survey, everyone has stopped making confident assertions.

And then, all of a sudden, things seem to be calming down. It's May 16th, and to tell the truth, when you just look out at the mountain, you get the feeling that not much is happening.

Some of the gawkers even start packing up and heading out.

As for those who had been evacuated early, they're asking if it's all right for them to go back home now, or at least, go back and grab a few things they forgot to pack, they won't be long, just a few items, and they'll be back at the shelter shortly. It's looking so calm up there that on the 17th, the officials relent, and say they'll allow people to go get their personal effects the next day around 10 a.m. So that's settled, everyone goes to bed, satisfied and reassured. In their little metal-frame cots lined up in the dormitory, they dream of this or that object, some souvenir or other, photographs (still silver prints back then?), a dress or jacket they'd like to have with them. And then, wouldn't it be nice to be back in the old homestead again, and anyway, don't you think the officials are making a big deal out of nothing, oh well, let's get some sleep so that we'll be in shape tomorrow.

Alarm clocks go off around eight. After a shower and breakfast, they figure they'll be ready to go. Arms come out from under the makeshift bedding, a stretch, a yawn and feet to the floor. For the next half-hour, they will still believe they are going home to get their stuff. A half-hour of happy anticipation mixed with a touch of grumpiness at having to drag themselves out of their cocoons, even for something they are looking forward to doing.

At 8:32, some are still in the shower, others having their coffee and looking out the window. And what they see, they're unlikely to ever forget.

The north face of the mountain collapses.

And it slides and slides, all that collapsing rock, moving at something like 150 mph, filling valleys and lakes with the nasty stuff, and to anybody or anything in its path, get your ass out of there.

In the shelters, they can't help but imagine: if they had planned an earlier departure, they'd have been in the middle of it, swept away, buried beneath the rubble, mouths full of ash. Those who aren't completely dumbstruck call out to the others, who come out of the showers still dripping and naked, with just a towel around their privates. *Jesus fuck*, words failed as they simply wagged their heads back and forth, like Parkinson's patients.

Fuck, Fred also says, already at his office and watching the whole thing unfold on screen, and he tries to reach David A. Johnston, who is thought to still be on the scene that morning, with his folding chair and binoculars.

Fred is someone I made up, he could be named anything, but there was certainly someone like him there, with those thoughts going through his head, the same concern, the same sense of urgency, as he tried to reach Johnston.

Magmatic gasses explode, hurling pumice and rock debris into a burning cloud. The heat is so tremendous that ponds evaporate, creeks and streams vanish into steam. There rises an immense column of ash, bearing crushed magma and dust, mud and vapor that the crater continues to spew for hours. The fallout adds to the flows that are already covering trails and prairies, forests and snowy slopes, glaciers. The rest is carried away by the winds.

The sky covers over and grows dark, and soon it looks like night in the middle of the day.

Winds continue to push the airborne debris eastward. The next day, over a thousand miles away, when people living in Boulder, Colorado wake up and look out at the sky, they'll find a cloud of ash hovering over their city, obscuring the main thoroughfare, where people will wander in a daze (the light in Boulder is famously brilliant). And the cloud will move on to circle the entire globe, thinning as it goes, dropping its mix of grayish particulate matter and water in varying concentrations, to be absorbed by the soil below.

But at present, tephra, pyroclastic flows and dacitic lava, Fred is in his office feverishly noting, while regularly attempting to reach David A. Johnston.

But David isn't answering.

Lahars are mudflows triggered by melting glaciers, thick, dense, fast-moving slurries that carry away everything in their path: tree trunks, bridges, houses that they break apart and grind into a lumpy paste. Lahars, scribbles Fred, still trying to get through by phone, as if he hadn't guessed by now what had happened, as if he refused to believe it, weak-kneed, his guts in a knot.

Vehicles are no match for a lahar either, and the one belonging to Reid Blackburn, caught in the flow, has nothing left to show but the roof and the gaping hole where the blown-out windshield once was. In pictures, you can see the steering wheel, and the door on the driver's side open.

I haven't said anything about Blackburn yet, a photographer

who'd been covering the volcano story for several papers. Unlike Johnston, he was a local boy, an Oregon native. He knew Mount St. Helens well, having climbed it, skied it, hiked it all his life. Down jacket and backpack, that was Blackburn's look. Big smile against a background of snowcapped mountains. Twenty-eight, recently married, he'd driven to within ten miles of the volcano so as not to miss the shot, in case the volcano erupted. And the flows rushed down the slope like an acid glue, densely packed and hot.

By the time everything had finally settled down, when the lahars had finished tearing up forests, plugging waterways, painting the land and a few unlucky individuals in a thick coat of gray mud, when the curls of ashen smoke that billowed above it all like endless entrails, twisting and bloated, started to disperse, when people finally dared lift their heads toward the quelled mountain, what they saw was no longer the mountain they'd known, the beautiful conical peak forever framed by their windows, no longer that regular, conventional shape that had always provided the town with its postcard-perfect background, reassuring in its familiarity. In its place, an amputee, a headless mountain.

Over twelve thousand fish had been blasted out of their streams. As for game animals, easily seven thousand animals, deer, moose, and bear—all either asphyxiated or burnt alive. Fifty-seven human lives were lost, including Johnston's and Blackburn's, while others' were forever changed as kin mourned their loss.

The culprit mountain, now weighed down by its sin, self-mutilated in a way, bore the stigmata of disaster on its own body. Afflicted in its appearance, shortened by some 1,300 feet, it now presented a flattened summit, above which spread a gaping sky.

The Sheriff Theory

STRETCHED OUT ON his bed in the little room at the Blueberry, on nights when he couldn't sleep, Colter would listen, just lie there and focus his ear, and attempt to identify, from the sound of their engines, the make and model of the few passing vehicles; he'd think about trips and travels, other places in the world.

And about the load of past and present that each driver was hauling along with him.

And then, there were the deep woodlands, endlessly enmeshed, extending all the way to Portland and down to the ocean. The untidy forest, overgrown and penumbral, where you never knew what might be lurking. And Colter would fall asleep to the notion of its boundlessness.

A forest with which the Louis and Clark expedition were well acquainted. They slept in it more often than they'd bargained for. Alders, ashes, white cedar, they knew them all. Groves of oak, where grouse and ocelot roamed. They etched their names into bark (any tree would do, cypress, pine, and fir, too), that the forest might rustle with the memory of their presence. That nature would long remember they'd once passed this way. They took to their penknives with gusto, signing everything in sight, as if they were the ones who'd sketched these landscapes.

What they actually did build were cabins, with tables and chairs, even chimneys; they were gifted, you have to admit. Confined to these lodgings during bad weather, they would infuse the buckthorn they'd picked (a thorny shrub whose leaves make a tea, though they say you should never eat the poisonous berries, even if birds and wild goats seem to enjoy the hallucinatory effects), and wait out the storm, dreaming of the hearth and home they'd left behind.

Colter's house, if you think about it, clouds must continue to scud across the sky above its three pediments and the birds that perch on the wires, composing their little melodic line, maybe a requiem, the first measures of a not-so-happy tune.

Colter had said that the wires were like a staff, which made the birds into notes, but you and me, we could just as easily say that the birds were little black socks hung out to dry on laundry lines, swinging bravely in the wind.

At this point, the house must be in pretty rough shape, open to the breeze, torn curtains slapping against the window frames and broken panes.

Colter revisited another thought, too, a pile he hadn't paid much attention to on that day he went back to the empty house, a heap next to the streetlamp outside that almost disappeared into the gloom of that wintery late afternoon. What else was in that pile, maybe two or three broken lamps, with their burnt shades, nothing much, a few other pieces of junk, dull and inert against the gray sky. And yet, there it was, sitting in the middle of it all, and this should have alerted him, the oversized stuffed tiger that had cost him an arm and a leg, the Christmas Eve when he'd brought it home, hugging it to his chest, full of daddy-pride in that early dusk that fell on the winter street, a big black and yellow plaything, too bulky, too cumbersome (the children preferred their small-scale animals, the ones that graced their beds and snuggled with them under the covers, though now, only one to each child, tucked safely under an arm, as we said) for the children to bring along with them, and now, coming unstitched, stuffing poking through the busted seams, the thing had been trashed, and must have watched them leaving like a decrepit pet dog that's being abandoned, too feeble to protest.

A few minutes after Colter had entered the deserted house, maybe at the same moment he fell unconscious to the carpeted floor in the living room, the streetlamp must have blinked on at its appointed hour, illuminating the wretched feline, splendid one last time, a final glory, before the garbage collectors passed at dawn and tossed it into the jaws of their compactor, grinding up the body with the rest of the day's debris.

Did it occur to Colter, from that little room where he was thinking about all this, did it ever occur to him, without Betty ever saying it, that one day, and maybe even several times, as they consistently failed to respond to eviction notices, that the sheriff had stopped by?

There she was, hanging around the house in her bathrobe when the knock came, demanding that she open. And there he'd be, striding into her house with the law on his side, standing there in the living room looking at Betty, so pretty with her hair let down and her bathrobe gaping. She wouldn't have thought to herself that it might be useful. Not even as a way to win him over; she might have done it instead out of sheer terror, a physical urge mixed with the desire to take her self-debasement as far as it would go. So she probably did nothing when he moved nearer. She was maybe even hoping he would, because of his size (Colter was on the small side), with that thirty-something smell of a guy who takes a shower every day, letting the water run as long as he wants, mixed with the day's sweat. And he could tell she wanted it, he must have unhooked the ties on the curtains, and let the heavy cotton drapery fall against the pane.

Maybe it had occurred to him, the possibility of something going on between Betty and the sheriff, as he slept in his little room at the Blueberry, all alone with the sound of passing cars and the forest that spread continuously to the ocean.

And at Moses's bar, too, he'd be ruminating, he'd get that scowl, you know, when his face would suddenly close up, focused on who knows what dark thoughts. Maybe he was thinking about the sheriff and Betty, of the flowered curtains she'd chosen for them, and which were supposed to protect their little family when night fell, or at least to balloon gloriously in the breeze, but not to act as a screen—they should have been simply filtering the sun's rays, softening the ambient light—to hide his wife's bare bottom offered up to the sheriff, now on his knees, taking care of business.

You can't help but imagine them, shielded from view by the flowered cotton drape, at first just standing there in the low light, him in uniform moving in on her, opening her terrycloth robe in a sudden gesture, revealing Betty's body—the sash came undone on its own, slipping to the floor like a dying eel. Her breasts, let's indulge ourselves a little, were now free, her full, silky pubic hair unveiled. The smell of Betty's sex was starting to waft through the room, and he thrust his fingers inside, didn't he, then down on his knees, inserted his tongue, quick and hungry, lacking method, before flipping Betty around to take her on all fours. All Betty saw now was the floor, up close, strands of carpet rocking back and forth like seas in a storm to the rhythm imposed by the sheriff, who pushed and shoved, grabbing her by the waist, until she felt her sex contract and come around the dick of the man who had shown up to tell her that her dream of the little house with hubby and kids was over.

One day, a little while later, after the sheriff had already paid several of his visits behind the flowered curtains, the very day Colter had found the house empty, maybe Betty had shown up at the sheriff's, with her two children clutching their teddy bears and a suitcase stuffed with everything she could manage to fit.

It's possible she had hoped it could happen, that he'd take all three of them under his wing, and that another kind of life would begin.

He would make a place for her in his life, is what she'd imagined, and he'd lean down and pick up her children, one after the other, lifting them off the earth, spinning them around the way they loved, way up high like an airplane, they would squeal, that game (I've never understood why they do that) everyone always plays with kids.

But the sheriff, when he saw this woman brimming with expectation (that look of hers, both pleading and fierce), when he sensed in her a weakness ever so slightly tinged with her indignity affixed to it, he acted as if nothing had ever happened between them.

He shifted his face into neutral, clenched his entire body, and tell me what your name is again, he said, in essence, and that he didn't know what she was talking about. Must be an eviction, he said, nodding toward the suitcase, feigning a guess; and yes, stuff happens, I've seen it a lot, but it's the law unfortunately (he kept repeating unfortunately), and never once did he inflect a single syllable with anything resembling kindness.

Then, over that expression she'd shown when first addressing him, that ambiguous look of anxious entreaty and defiance, there fell something like a veil. Her lusterless eyes now conveyed nothing but bewilderment and resignation. Gone was the bold and watchful gaze on the cusp of decision. She had been drained of something essential, her face emptied, her color gone suddenly pale; an illegible blankness had replaced the lively complexity of her feelings in a matter of seconds, and despondency set in as she conceded defeat.

Even at this moment, as he stood there pretending not to recognize her, claiming to confuse her with all the other women to whom he'd had to issue eviction warrants, even then, with his massive body barricaded behind a lie, the sheriff still looked so good to her. Betty's lifeless eyes, still anxious to come away with something, grazed the creases of his cotton uniform, and she pictured everything that was underneath, the truth of the sheriff's body, how hairy and where, the exact color of his nipples, the love handles, everything she'd had time to contemplate on the afternoons of his visits, when beads of sweat would cling to the hair on his chest. Then, she grasped in one hand the pull-out handle of her suitcase, and in the other, the hand of her youngest, who was holding his older brother's in his other, and she turned and walked away, straight ahead (was she improvising at this point, or did she have a plan B?), because there was no way, after all this, that she would ever see Colter again.

The sheriff didn't close the door right away, but watched her leave, her back turned, the two kids in tow. An ant was climbing up the doorframe, and he crushed it with his thumb.

The Seagull

EVERY SO OFTEN, let me put it this way, I'd wonder if I'd seen something, and I don't mean ants, which I'm pretty sure were there, but another critter, a little cockroach, at Moses's place, I do believe that's what it was, a little roach that lived its little roach life while we were there talking, that kind of thing happens, crawling along the bar, or scuttling around Colter's feet, or Shannon's (it's reluctant to climb up a shoe, better not, too risky, safer to go around it), before heading to the back of the barroom, where it's calmer, a couple of empty tables and chairs (room for ghosts, if ghosts are looking for company); and the bug catches its breath, the way I imagine it, secure in the dark corner, far from the noisy folks up front that it's not sure are dangerous or otherwise, but caution is the better part of valor, you can't be too careful with those bodies that are thousands of times yours in volume, best wait until everyone's gone to find your way back to the bar in search of any crumbs that might have escaped the vigilance of Moses's sponge, which isn't as fussy as his towel for wiping glasses, but still, it's something, thinks the little roach that has started to get used to the bar's comings and goings.

Anyway, it seemed to me that there was one of those critters crawling around some evenings, but it could have just been a shadow, some movement seen out of the corner of the eye, a reflection, something there and gone in a flash. I didn't give it any further thought.

In the damp but cozy smell of Moses's bar (nothing like the moldy smell of his childhood home, water seeping into the cement walls that would stain, bulge, and blister, the fungus that must have been proliferating in there), that mix of beer fumes with the exhalations from the ocean nearby (very different, thought Colter, from the sour stench of the foundationless house where he managed to survive the first sixteen years of his life between mother and fake father) (and did something tip him off back then, if you don't mind my raising this here, regarding the fake father, without his putting it in so many words; I mean, something more than just that feeling of strangeness you always get at one point or another of your childhood or teen years, you know, the adoption fable, you must have asked yourself at some point, right? Everyone does, so he must have made up some story as to why the father wasn't really his, all the while believing that, of course, he had to be), in that air heavy with salt and hops, iodine and barley, Colter tried to piece himself back together.

He must have been obsessing over where Betty ended up, what city, with his children, who were growing up without him. Or was he trying to erase them from memory, to lock them up in some dank dungeon of the mind, the one where he'd sequestered the image of his dead mother, and fake father, and also, since that was something Colter never spoke of, the enigma of the true one?

   All of them, each in their own way, had abandoned him, and his whole life was nothing but a string of abandonments. Ever since he was little, people were figuring out ways to leave him behind.

Every time I look up and see the ocean, and think of all the stories I've heard at Moses's place, I can't help making an uncanny connection between the useless, violent spectacle of the surf pounding the strand and the way fate has gone about methodically crushing whatever chance for happiness Colter and the others ever stood.

Because fate didn't seem to have finished with them yet. There was always one more humiliating trick in the bag.

The worst thing about these guys was that they'd come to believe they were living discount lives, that they'd drawn a really lousy ticket in life's lottery. But they would have to make do with the bum hand they'd been dealt. Which is what they did, drowning their idle daylight hours in cheap beer, telling themselves that the sun would rise again, and wasn't that just grand, Harry Dean would ask, that the sun was going to come up and lift the landscape out of its murky midnight and bring color back into the world. And they would all drink to that, clinking their mugs to the dawning of a new day, to the rising sun, and they'd swallow the insult of their daily existence, their broken childhoods and what came next, which was nothing to brag about, even though they'd tried their best, because they did try their best, they hadn't always been cruel fate's passive victims: there were those times when they gave it all they had, Shannon recalled, but it seemed every time they thought they'd finally made it out of the woods, that they'd achieved the dream (house with a family inside), it would all unravel, and once the wives had become mothers, they forgot the wife part of the deal, and then the money would run out for all sorts of reasons, and finally the whole thing would go down the drain, even the love, not through any one person's fault, and the little they'd gained would be gone.

How do you explain the rule that when you've finally ended a losing streak, when you've almost erased even the memory of all your rotten luck, and you settle at last into what I'll call a fresh, triumphant now, how come the curse suddenly returns, Colter asked anyone within earshot, raising his mug in the moist air. Or maybe not a curse, conceded Colter, but man, it sure feels like one. And Shannon and the other guys nodding their heads as if they were actually turning over in their minds the issue of how to deal with the obstinacy of events to conspire against the peaceful life you're trying to build.

That's what it felt like at Moses's bar (Moses who, by the way, never said anything, though I can tell you there was a lot going on in there), all the stories they lugged around like unwieldy baggage, all the messes they left in their wake, for all to see.

And that's what the kid in the picture was looking at, the unwieldy baggage, as these guys sat at the bar carrying on their shaggy rant, their ideas going wherever the alcohol led and soon, this is how it seemed to me, racing ahead of the speaker's ability to put them into words—those of us listening would be panting to keep up (I don't know about the others, but speaking for myself, I found I was often taunted by some idea that would turn a corner and vanish, as I tried to get words to stick to it and make sense, but the tease kept fleeing ahead, egging me on). We were a pretty sorry-looking bunch by the end of the night, and maybe that was what flashed in the retinas of the kid in the picture, maybe it was us all along.

When I couldn't bear the kid's eyes anymore, I'd go out onto the stoop for a smoke. The windows across the way were often still lit. In the distance, you could just make out the fencing that runs out to the horizon, looking frail and vulnerable in the dark.

These guys' lives, in a sense, I would be out there thinking, at night in the cold, and I thought to myself, to sum them up (and I often think the same thing when I'm sitting and staring out my window), it's more like they were reading their lives than writing them. It's like they were discovering each episode of their stories one by one, as it was happening, but couldn't do anything about it. Like someone had decided in advance how things were going to turn out, a dark force at work. And try as they might to make use of whatever latitude they still had, the next episode would always come like a bolt from the blue.

Out there on the stoop, I could hear the muzzy sound

of the ocean as it labored to and fro on the same beach I'm gazing at now. Out here, thank you much, there are no pelicans dive-bombing for fish, only seagulls that occasionally cross my sightline outside the window. You might argue that they also have a few killings on their conscience, and any fish that ventures too near the surface risks just as much here (swimming along, unsuspecting, up where the light plays so prettily on the water), as in Long Beach, where a fish is liable to be cut down in its hour of glory by those ruthless, sharp-beaked hunters. The seagulls do their business at surface level, though, with their sensibly proportioned beaks, producing less of a spectacle, and therefore provoking less outcry. Plus, they have that friendly way of begging humans for food. They know how to make themselves understood. One used to come visit me in the early days, wanting, it seemed, to engage me in conversation. It would get my attention with a clumsy dance of seduction, standing first on one leg, then the other, eyeing me with head tilted, plunging its round-eyed gaze into mine in the hope of somehow stirring me to action.

I was on the verge of giving it a name.

When I went back inside, I saw the kid was still there, with his smile too big to be true, distress written all over his face. What must have been so scary back when this shot was taken was the boy's future that opened up before him like a bottomless pit (the lot of children, feeble, inchoate creatures that stand quivering on the threshold of the unknown; don't they have every reason to waver before the gaping abyss at their feet?). That's what you could read on the face, if that's who it was, of little Moses B. Reed, thumbtacked to the wall behind the bar, the forced smile, since the camera was aimed at him and he had to fake it, pretend to be happy whenever one of his parents clicked on the shutter, while the reverse shot from the child's viewpoint was the baggy monster, shapeless and looming, the specter of times to come.

And the grown-up Moses, hour after hour behind his bar,

who seemed to be saying to the boy Since you're wondering, just look, this is now, nothing complicated about it. Moses posted that picture there so that the child could stop wondering, stop fearing, so that his question would finally be answered, and he could look out at this day-to-day routine and see the tidy, almost peaceful existence of the adult he had become.

For those future times had come, and they were now, and in a way, the child had been right to fear them, because of everything that they all had lost, all of them sitting there, and as for Moses, none of them knew that when he'd lie down to sleep in his studio above the bar, and his hand reached for the cord on his table lamp with the fringed shade, none of them knew whether this wasn't just what he'd always dreamed for himself (despite having to stand there for hours at a time), just as they knew next to nothing about all the rest. Moses, who, in order to get to his bed at night, in high summer, and I can't remember who told me this, had to walk through a curtain of flypaper ribbons that hung in strips like a curtain with the little fly corpses stuck all over it, what's a guy supposed to say about that? And he'd fall asleep, mouth open, among the forest of sticky ribbons where unsuspecting flies would get their little legs caught and slowly expire, leaving behind dry husks that dotted each ribbon like an embroidered motif.

And that's not counting the pink plastic flyswatter with a flexible handle left on the nightstand, in the event that he woke in the middle of the night, alerted by a dipteran craftier than the others that managed to evade the ribbons and buzz by the sleeping Moses, who'd grab the weapon, half-awake now, to crush the little beast, which would either let itself be slain, blindsided by such violence, or, figuring it had best not stick around, would have flown off in the nick of time, just as the arm was rising, warned by the displaced air that it had better hightail out of there if it valued its own life.

Moses's Uncle

It was mid-winter, with a weird kind of snow suspended in the air, tiny, shrunken flakes that thickened the atmosphere and made it hard to breathe. I'd walked to the *Ulysses* through the empty streets, short of breath, feeling almost like I was suffocating.

It was snowing that night, yes, I remember vividly how it was falling in limp, persistent flakes, and Harry Dean must have balked at the idea of taking the truck out, of driving on slippery pavement with snowflakes coming at the windshield as if united into a single force bent upon crushing themselves on the glass like a swarm of insects, and you squinting into the blurry light, trying to remain vigilant as the flakes dance in your headlights—a kind of hypnosis that can set in when you drive in the snow. He'd left Colter to fend for himself that night, maybe turn in early, and there he'd be, stretched out on the bed, sensing the creeping cold outside the window, imagining the snow falling so relentlessly in the vast night, clinging to pine branches, blanketing the parking lot with an even layer, each fragile new flake joining its fellows on the blacktop.

As for Shannon, even the couple hundred yards he had to walk would look like an endless trek in these conditions, and he decided to stay in the cocoon of his apartment, curled up with Mary (let's not even mention Tim, who came so rarely anyway that he wasn't about to show up on a nasty night like this, no way).

So, do the math, it was just Moses and me that night, inside the woody dampness of the bar, snow falling hard as ever outside, while inside felt darkly, imperfectly secure.

Moses served me up a beer, and I was having trouble striking up conversation.

The child in the photo was gauging my silence, and I felt like asking Moses a question about it, a question about what the child was afraid of, about where such a legible fear could be coming from, and the basic question as to why the picture was there in the first place, night after night, sending some kind of warning, what were we to make of this little oracle, always to his back, of this strange apprenticeship between the child and his adult self, this unnatural, spectral presence that he kept by his side.

But nothing came, not even the start of a sentence, and not just because I had to find the words in English.

So, I thought (as a refuge, I had to think about something, rather than sit there in stony silence, mine as well as Moses's) about the men of the Lewis and Clark expedition slowly pushing ahead in the snow (since there must have been snow at some point during their westward trek), feet numb with cold, backs bent with exhaustion. About them gazing from inside their makeshift huts at the falling flakes.

If you look closely, you'll see that not all flakes fall, strictly speaking. There are those that flit and flutter, catching some air current or other, and they're suddenly waltzing to and fro, breaking free from the stupidly obedient troops that fall straight down, as if it were a chore, a task to be carried out in blind obedience without deviation. It must have been mind-boggling to watch those renegade flakes, their eyes dazed by so much heedlessness, to follow the swirling course of those magnificently carefree crystals that took all the time in the world before finally coming to earth.

The snow, overall, you can be fairly sure they weren't thrilled about it. The chapped lips, the frostbite, your packs soaked and heavy, put yourself in their place, and all that whiteness, sure, it's pretty for a while, but in the end, it would start to drive you a little nuts.

Yes, in the end, they were craving color.

I mean, picture it: once everything had gone white—grass, rocks, soil, and clay—once the snow had blanketed absolutely everything in sight, nature was nothing but a blank page, all relief and color erased. And the famished, snow-blinded men looked out upon the blankness; and in their hearts, another emptiness settled in, a feeling of utter destitution, as if they'd been stripped of all they possessed: the land in all its many contours, all the shades of green normally on display in nature, all suffocating now beneath a thick white layer, banished from sight.

So much so that the sky joins in. If it weren't for the ruddy faces of their fellow explorers, each would swear that the whole world had been drained of color.

Through the rectangle of windows roughly hewn amid the logs of their hastily erected cabin walls, this was all they could see, nature rendered null and void, beyond reach, congealed in whiteness. The great outdoors rendered impractical.

You'd think nature had wanted to keep us out, had developed this strategy to prevent humans from trudging through. Like certain species of octopus that transform themselves to dissuade predators, nature invented snow, thick and cumbersome. The expedition team simply looked on, baffled. (As for singing nature's praises and exalting at the notion of symbiosis, that was hardly their concern.)

It's understandable that so many animals opt for hibernation. Roll into a ball in some burrow and wait it out, nothing to think about until it's time to hit the road again, I'll bet some of those men dreamt of nothing more.

Color and line are not the only things erased by the snow, but sound as well. The whole world, listen closely, and you get the feeling the world has been shrouded in soundproofing. When they venture out, it's like walking on cotton. It's soft, giving way beneath the foot without the usual thud that steps make. The best you can get in terms of acoustic interaction with the outdoors is a crunch. And the men sent out to hunt anyway (it's all they can do to bag a crow off a bare tree branch, since the rest of creation is hibernating a hundred feet underground—intractable nature keeping it all to herself) trudge on in silence, with only the rubbing of the shoe that sinks into the cold, crumbly matter of this white desert. They miss the accompaniment, the confirmation of their physical existence that the sound of their soles provides, you know what I mean, when you walk on a hard surface that makes your steps resonate to your personal rhythm, your interior cadence, heels naturally beating time to your music.

The thin layer of snow sticking to my overcoat melted slowly and formed little puddles on the floor, evaporating lazily, leaving dark spots on the wooden planks that would be gone by the next day.

The child with the anxious smile was still emitting a vibe of unresolved fear into the room, with that toothy smile of children who've yet to lose their baby teeth. In fact, if you got close up (I leaned over the bar a little while Moses was getting something from the pantry), was it just a shadow, or was there actually a tooth missing; so maybe that was it, the child was afraid to smile because of the big gap in his grin, the raw memory of holding the little tooth in his hand, of realizing that you can lose things just like that, these little parts of the self to be mourned, the bloody incisor that was tossed out, in the end.

It was Moses himself who ended up taking the first step.

Something stood between us, Moses and me, something that went beyond the language barrier, beyond the fact that he'd spent his whole life between Portland and Cannon Beach, while

I came from somewhere else altogether, maybe the material reality of the bar itself, a literal boundary that staked out our respective territories and doomed us to remain in our sealed spaces, which is what happened, wasn't it, night after night, Moses entrenched behind his counter, with only that frail little child to lean on, the child, like some open wound, looking fraught, ready for the worst, while Moses stood in isolation, authoritative, tight-lipped and straining to repress his thoughts by wiping his mugs over and over, in an attempt to tame his inner voice, to put it to sleep, that's right, my pretty, singing sweet lullabies to his demons, that they might settle down and nod off instead of swirling around him like furies.

Once he'd figured that no one else was going to show, Moses filled a couple of mugs and came around to the other side of the bar and motioned with his shoulder for me to come join him at one of the back tables.

And that's how I came to be sitting next to Moses, having a drink, elbow to elbow, a situation that has not recurred since.

He must have figured out that I was the only one who stared at that photo every night, wondering what made that smile seem the opposite of joy. Is that why he wanted to confide in me, this man of so few words, forever wiping his beer mugs as if it was his own past he was trying to erase? Searching for spots, as if they symbolized something, though no one ever really knew what it was he felt so driven to blot out, night after night; and it was far from clear that the story of his uncle (because that's what he told me that night, the story of his uncle) resolved the mystery.

Anyway, here's what he told me.

Moses was seven, and his father would sometimes take him up Mount St. Helens to burn off some of that little kid energy. Because that's what Sundays looked like in those parts. You got up, dragged your feet a while, wondering how you were going to spend this vacant, purposeless day, with no schedule to adhere to, and then you'd look out the window and there it stood, good old Mount St. Helens to the rescue. You'd grab your picnic baskets, head into the outdoors, and start up the trails. Mount St. Helens was always synonymous with hiking, botanizing and bird-watching, where you could hear the crisp flapping of a marsh tit's wings, catch sight of a firecrest in flight, and will you look at that Bohemian waxwing, with its orange tuft. Once you were pretty high up, you could look back out on where you lived. You could pinpoint your own house, so small at this distance, down at the foot of the mountain.

Until May 18, 1980, when everything turned sour.

In the house, tiny when seen from above, but big enough at ground level, Moses's uncle, since he's the one we're talking about here, at 8:30, on that same May 18th, was among the locals who were having a leisurely breakfast by their window. At 8:31, still nothing, alone at the table, the uncle was calmly eating his muffins with blueberry jam and a drop of maple syrup. And then, it was 8:32.

When he saw the explosion, all that rock flying into the air, the thick column of ash that rose like some epic event in the otherwise placid sky, he ran out into the yard and kept running.

He got nearer and nearer to the mountain, to see things close up.

He spent hours out there, getting still closer, breathing the noxious air beneath the epic sky choked with smoke and cinder, in awestruck disbelief at what was happening.

He didn't return at nightfall.

His legs were collapsing under him.

Then, the idea of a bed, cotton sheets, his bedroom, all that suddenly seemed unbearably narrow and constraining.

He found a hollow in the terrain where he lay down, right

on the ground, exhaustion winning out over discomfort.

When he woke up, everything was calm.

The landscape had gone lunar, ashen, unrecognizable.

The uncle felt as if he'd awoken thousands of miles from home. It was like the soil of some distant planet, a new frontier to be explored.

Robinson Astronaut, or whatever story he was narrating in his head, he wandered the barren land, nothing familiar in sight. He spent days on the mountain, barely alive, without food, a stranger in a strange land.

It didn't take long, however, for the volcano to repopulate.

Not only were helicopters hovering everywhere in search of bodies or survivors, but the uncle ran into people who were coming in to dig through the debris, uncover things they could resell, objects left behind in the destroyed homes that they could pull out of the rubble.

The uncle knew then that it was time to get out of there.

But go home, no way. Once you've seen the place where you've picnicked a hundred times covered over in a thick gray sludge that carried away everything in its wake (trees, houses and the people in its path), and later, the human vultures coming to sift through the ash, no respect for the dead, no, after that, you can't go back to life as usual.

The uncle pushed deeper into the wilderness.

He walked along riverbeds where the water had evaporated, or where the cooling lava, like nature's concrete, had dammed up the water's flow, he cut a path through upended trunks, going around or climbing over, stopping occasionally to rest on a charred stump, a small, breathless but living thing amidst such massive devastation.

All around him, fractured, disjointed trees, some cracked

right in half, others with open wounds bleeding sap; tissue torn, vessels ripped out, fibers cut clear or rough, looking like whale baleens, thousands of living beings vivisected, the smell of death hanging over this arboreal killing field.

The uncle ended up walking so far that he eventually came upon relatively unscathed forests.

Ash still clung to the leaves, and there was an odd mud mixture underfoot, composed of soil and rain-borne cinder and ash; but the trees were still standing, however dusty and lusterless.

As if the forest had grown old overnight, gone suddenly gray, the way people's hair can sometimes turn white after a fright.

The uncle trekked on through this alien landscape until he found clean, green leaves, walkable trails, and drivable roads.

There, he hitchhiked a ride, and kept pushing further and further away, stopping when someone offered him some menial job or other, helping out here or there, moonlighting, as it were.

The Reeds thought for a long time that the volcanic eruption had killed their uncle.

Moses had gotten that far into his story, but our mugs were empty, so he went back to the bar for a refill. I don't know why I started thinking about having to walk back to the motel in the snow, about the sidewalks that would be completely covered now in inches of the white stuff where my feet would be cutting a path, leaving a trace.

The Story of the Uncle, Continued

I COULD HEAR the beer pouring from the tap, I imagined how alone the uncle must have been in that gray wasteland, and my thoughts digressed to the Louis and Clark expedition team again. Bogged down in all that whiteness, they must have been on the lookout for any sign of spring, pinning their hopes to the slightest hint, the tiniest growth on a branch that might suggest a first budding. As if they could imagine the slow labor of germination taking place under the snow. They pictured all the life going on underneath, everything brewing down there, bravely battling so that one day, it might exist above ground. And from these silent, invisible struggles being waged several dozen inches under their worn-out soles, they drew strangely powerful inspiration. The prospect of the imminent thaw, the return to a landscape of greenness and warmth, must have glimmered on the horizon of these men's every thought, delirious as they were from so long a vigil.

Moses returned with the mugs of beer, and the uncle ended up in a cute little town, cuter than most, where the streets gave off a frivolous, benign air, the harmless breeze brushed the freshly painted storefronts and houses and tickled the petals of the geraniums that graced the window-boxes of every facade. Then, all of a sudden (his memory of them had all but disappeared, first as a thing he confusedly sought to flee, and then, inexplicably, they vanished completely from his mind, leaving a void, a gaping emptiness), he remembered those he'd left behind at the house, who must have thought he'd died.

Out in front of the grocery store, there was a revolving

postcard stand sunning itself (as he twirled it around, it made a sound he hadn't heard in so long, remember, that squeak so evocative of summer holidays), and he picked one out, a doctored sunset, big orange ball plunging into the dark sea, garnet-colored streaks against a flaming sky.

On the flip side (sitting in a fashionable pub a while later, tucked into a booth against a thick-glassed ochre window that seemed filled with little bubbles, like someone exhaling underwater), he wrote that he was all right, or something like that, and that they shouldn't wait for him, Don't wait for me, okay, and he slapped a stamp on it and sent it to the ones who would find it one morning in their cylindrical roadside mailbox affixed to its upright post, looking like some wading bird, who themselves had not yet made sense of what had happened.

What is sure is that the eruption had changed a great deal in everyone's hearts.

There were some, perhaps, like the uncle, for whom the volcano had brought certain things into perspective. Some felt a strange symbiosis with the eruption, where the volcano's awakening somehow triggered their own. The mountain everyone had always relied on had exploded out of boredom, and didn't this sudden outburst mean that even the most stable elements in the universe could be modified? The uncle had run out of the house, as if summoned by the volcano, called to rise from his lethargy. He would have been at a loss to explain, even to himself, why this empty moonscape that the mountain had wrought made him keep running, further from home. It just seemed obvious to him that he was being issued an order by the furious mountain. It took this event for him to realize that he'd spent his entire life dragged into all sorts of situations without ever wondering whether or not he should be there. He took other people's advice, out of sheer inertia, as if he were somehow destined to follow in their footsteps, to go down the path forged by those with a greater sense of purpose. Did this passiveness on his part (the uncle, sitting on the decapitated stump, was asking himself this question amid the smell of slowly cooling ash) account for his sense that his life had been lived without him? Suddenly, his existence back at the house seemed like a delusion, like someone else's life. So now, in synchrony with nature, with the landscape in upheaval, he hit the road, in search of what, he knew not, something most probably within himself that life in the house had been suppressing, or making it impossible to access.

Most of the folks living around there were still thunder-struck, hurting to the core. After their long and uneventful acquaintance with the volcano, so peaceful that they thought of it as nothing but a mountain, the sudden frenzied unleashing, the senseless aggression by the most familiar of sceneries, the sudden transformation of a kindly, welcoming mountain into a ferocious volcano—how can nature be so two-faced, presenting its bucolic wonders, from its wildflowers to its snowy ski slopes that made you feel so alive, and then out of nowhere, turn into a death machine? You couldn't trust anything anymore.

The eruption blew the whole summit right off, taking a number of lives with it, but it also obliterated people's confidence in the landscape, their sense of solid ground underfoot, an uncomplicated anchoring to a place that defined them, the unwritten covenant that binds people's everyday lives to the space they inhabit.

In the hearts of those who chose to stay, who didn't use the cataclysm as an excuse to flee, the eruption had another enduring effect, including for those who didn't personally know any of the fifty-seven lava victims, whose personal ties and relationships remained essentially intact: a new fragility, a nagging uncertainty, an awful fear of being suckered again.

It was against this background, the feeling of having been conned by a volcano, that Moses's uncle's relatives received his postcard.

They had long since given up hope of ever again seeing the uncle alive.

They would talk about him sometimes, in the evening on the big sofa in front of the television that was still working, in spite of it all, and their tears would mix with all kinds of belated praise for a man they hadn't appreciated enough back when they were living together.

So, when they saw the postcard, eyes wide in disbelief, they were at first over the moon with joy at this resurrection.

But that joy lasted only a few seconds before they came around to the harsh fact that the uncle didn't want to come home.

And just as they felt betrayed by old daddy mountain that had always been the town's distant figurehead, whose slopes were always available for sports and leisure, a picture-perfect view through every window, a familiar figure that people had grown strangely attached to, and that was now nothing but a shattered mass, self-destructing while destroying everything else in the process, undermining the people's trust, they also felt just as betrayed by the uncle.

They wavered between joy at knowing he was alive and a deep resentment.

They resented having mourned him for nothing, entire evenings in tears, when whole swathes of your life disappear as you fall into that listless stupor of pain, insensitive to the passage of time.

But something else was coming over them, slowly eating away at them, something harder to deal with.

As if in empathy with the uncle, who ran out and left them alone in the house (which seemed amputated of a member, now that he was gone), scorned and useless, limping through life in the shadow of this contempt he seemed to feel toward them (they, who weren't good enough for him, apparently, whose company he didn't seem to miss enough to justify coming back), as if they couldn't help concluding he must be right, they started to feel (it was a dull, surreptitious ache, hard to fully account for) that creeping sense of self-loathing.

Because, in families, there's always one who wants to leave, who believes the grass is greener somewhere else, on the far side of the mountain, who leaves the others behind in shocked disbelief to fend for themselves, convinced they didn't measure up; because that's the way it always happens, they're not only left on their own, wishing you hadn't gone away, but also, and you should have thought this through before leaving everyone in the lurch, they go and blame themselves for not being good enough.

Which is why this out-of-the-blue, unhoped-for sign from a revenant, this postcard with its huge sun sinking into the dark abyss of the ocean, felt more like a slap in the face than anything else. What were they to do with it? They couldn't set it on the mantle like a greeting card, or just toss it, or what about stuffing it into a drawer, and that's what they did, they slipped it into a pile of papers where it became invisible, as stale mail often does, hidden in plain sight, and that's the last time we'll mention it, do you understand, I don't want to hear his name spoken in this house, ever again.

It was a long time before Moses spoke the name again. He'd buried it with all the other inexplicable things reflected in the gaze of that child in the photograph thumbtacked to the wall behind him, taken perhaps on the day that he and everybody else saw the ash cloud rising into the Portland sky, things like the uncle's disappearance that same day, his vanishing into thin air, and you, Moses, had every reason to believe he was killed by that plume, asphyxiated, burnt alive in the lava. Or a different scenario, if the snapshot was taken several months later (that is, after the uncle's postcard landed in the one-legged mailbox— heron or flamingo, as you wish—that swallowed it like a fish, gulp, before regurgitating it into the hands of the horrified addressee—I mean, let's face it, the uncle was pretty rude, running away like that, playing dead, treating them all like dirt), the idea that he was actually alive somewhere in the forests, wandering alone in unimaginable conditions, and wouldn't be coming back: the thought that he'd just left them to their own devices, and how the furious gaze of the father behind the camera conveyed these feelings while imprinting the film with the frightened smile of a child whose uncle, his father's own brother, felt no need to see growing up.

Our mugs were empty again, the bar silent and stuffy, and I wondered when the youngster Moses had for the last time spent some casual family time with his uncle, maybe a few days before the eruption, or even the night before, rolling his little toy truck between his uncle's slippers while the man tried to read his newspaper, vaguely annoyed that the kid was playing underfoot, a moment in time innocent of what loomed on the horizon, not the slightest premonition that it would be their last.

Perry's Departure

So MANY THINGS I still need to tell you before getting to what has been my main concern from the start, so many things to explain, for example, how I ended up coming into possession of the two tomes of the Lewis and Clark expedition (and gave them a read, to add to what Harry had already told me), because it was Harry Dean himself who gave them to me one night, and I'm not sure, when I think about it, when I try and figure it all out, if he was trying to reach out to me somehow that night, or if it was just Harry's way of getting rid of the two volumes, which he had no intention of reading, one way or the other.

And how Harry came to have the books, well, that was Perry, of course, who'd left them for him, because one day, Perry just up and left the farm.

And if we're going to tell that episode, the one about Perry leaving, since everything matters in this story, we can start with this, with the fact that, for Perry, even the name of Mildred had become like a poison.

Because that's just what happened.

The name Mildred had become like a poison.

All Perry had to do was say it out loud (or even to himself, while daydreaming, when the name would surface all by itself, unsolicited) for him to suddenly go numb: his thoughts would stutter and freeze, his body would grow suddenly heavy, sluggish, as if some toxic liquid were coursing through his veins, a substance that his extensive drives through the surrounding area were intended to purge.

Every morning, Perry would get back into his beat-up, mud-splattered used car, his chunky notebook resting on the passenger seat, and off he'd go, wheels in the footsteps of Lewis and Clark and the men they'd brought along, each with his own personal story whose details will remain forever unknown to us. Each with his particular reason for setting off, leaving kin on the dock one cold afternoon as they boarded their ship, and all united in their readiness to grapple with whatever nature could throw at them, whether danger or deprivation, the harshness of nature in its vastness, or that rain, damn it, which hadn't let up a moment since they arrived in Oregon territory.

Because you have to talk about what happens when the snow starts to melt. You think the worst is over, that you'll finally be hitting the trail and getting enough to eat. But the rains bring our men to a halt once again. And sometimes rain turns to hail. The soft, syrupy sound that suggests the notion of wetness gives way to short, sharp, staccato taps, an arrhythmic drumming.

Still, Perry drove through this country, with rain beating down on his car roof, or other times hail, and he experienced a sense of continuity with those men, who somehow compensated, in his imagination anyway, for Mildred's absence.

Mildred: I wonder what she looked like.

I don't know why, but I picture her wearing a hat; pale-skinned, slender and delicate, blushing at the slightest emotion, eyes a porcelain blue. Something old-fashioned about her, and behind her seeming shyness was someone who was making her way in life, strong-willed and unsparing, the callousness of youth that has yet to experience life's trials, and who guards against them through her boundlessly avenging self-centeredness.

All Perry saw was the blue-eyed, pale-skinned fay, and didn't suspect the iron will that lay concealed beneath the sweetly bland exterior until it had turned against him.

Almost overnight, he was no longer welcome, and since nothing was ever explained, Perry's questions went unanswered, swimming back and forth in his mind like nervous fish in an aquarium, darting every which way within the watertight parameters that kept them separate from the outside world.

If it so happened, and I'm saying this because I'm also thinking about Colter and his empty house, if it just so happened (and even statistically, I realize how slim the chances are that it did), Mildred had met Betty. In her wanderings, children in tow, Betty would have been pushing further east, reversing the ancestors' trek, into more civilized lands, she might have been saying to herself, ending up in the city where Perry and Mildred lived, St. Louis, Missouri.

Imagine the scene, Betty sitting with her kids in some fast-food place where she'd spend her hard-earned cash (what low-paying, dead-end job had she managed to find) on a festive Sunday lunch, and Mildred, who was stopping by for a burger, that day when Perry was busy doing who knows what, some prior commitment, and had failed to make time to see her. Maybe Mildred sat at the same table as Betty, struck up a conversation, and ended up writing down her phone number, in case she ever needed help.

They might have gotten together every so often. Mildred (and feel free to disagree with me on this point) could well have been moved by Betty's story, and soon after, this is how I imagine it, by the same body that had aroused the sheriff. The longer she looked at Betty, the more Mildred wondered how you'd go about it with that kind of body, having a vague idea already, based on her own. And the two of them, Mildred, who was still with Perry, and Betty, who had loved Colter and the sheriff, and maybe others as well, may have tried out some gentle things together, or even some more daring things, but all perfectly delightful. In the end, Mildred left Perry, for no apparent reason, as we have learned, without mentioning Betty—it was none of his business—and brought Betty and the kids to live at her place, where they cuddled and made endless sixty-nine love, fill in whatever blanks you'd like.

What's certain, in any case, is that Perry woke up one morning in his little room on the farm, unrefreshed after a night of uneven, grimly determined sleep, one of those stippled sleeps, you've been there, where you doggedly attempt to plunge back into a dream when something (a noise? a thought?) keeps dragging you back to the surface. The gray dawn seeped through a gap in the curtains, bouncing feebly off the facing wall before falling onto the sorry-looking carpet where the pale ray cast its cool light on the two Lewis and Clark tomes that lay supine on the floor.

Perry eventually got up and went down to the kitchen and made himself some pancakes (E-Z style, a mix where you only add water and stir, you can't miss, before pouring the mixture onto the hot griddle), which he ate, sitting at the oilcloth-covered table, looking out occasionally onto the large, colorless barnyard that reflected into the equally colorless sky.

On that day, Perry's face seemed unusually focused, something intense and determined about it, almost arrogant, that would have made any encounter with a person who chanced to enter the room extremely unpleasant: you felt that, behind the resolute visage, something dangerous was brewing that might explode if anyone dared speak.

He went back up to his room (if we'd been at the farm, we would have heard him rummaging around up there), and in no time at all, he was back downstairs with a bag slung over his back and his two Lewis and Clark books, which he left on the kitchen table, with a note, For Harry.

He dropped by the Blueberry to say goodbye to Wendy. It's unlikely they talked about his reasons for leaving. Or whether he'd found what he'd been looking for. Or whether the whole trip suddenly looked to him like a woefully inadequate attempt at forgetting Mildred, when all it did was worsen the pain, as each tree, each breaking wave reminded him he was there because of her. Every breakfast at the farm, every night spent in the upstairs bedroom, hoping for the deliverance of sleep.

Wendy watched him through the bay window as he walked out to his car. He opened the driver side door, and she saw him fold into the seat. A truncated man now, framed by the side window like a portrait in profile.

The car started up, taking with it the miniature portrait, and that was the last Wendy heard of Perry.

The Bus Trip

IF PERRY LEFT, and we talked about this with Harry the night he brought me the two books about the Lewis and Clark expedition, it was most likely because he'd pretty much seen everything he'd come to see, all the landscapes and backcountry where the men had trekked, and he considered his investigation complete. Maybe he left with the feeling that none of this had served any purpose, regarding the Mildred issue, and that, since he'd been unable to forget her, he might as well just go home. But then again, maybe it was just the reverse, because of an incident involving him, which he told Harry about later.

Oh, it's an incident that, on its own, has little to do with my story here, but now that you've gotten to know Perry a little, it might interest you to know more about what he was going through emotionally while he was driving around the region. And it's an anecdote we all stand to profit from, a little boost, you might say, when it comes to matters of love.

Here's what it's all about.

That day, something was wrong with Perry's car, so rather than lose a whole day, he decided to take the bus that makes stops on the road that runs along the farm; that way, he was able to stay on the trail of his two heroes. Duly noted: he got on the bus, picked a seat, slipped his notebook into the net pouch affixed to the back of the seat in front of him, rested his temple against the sort of antimacassar (large rectangle of white cotton, a bit wrinkled, attached to the garnet velveteen seat cover with Velcro), and with his face thus turned toward the window, our Perry gazed out at the landscape that was starting to move as the bus inched forward.

It's entertaining to ride a bus, a little like watching a movie, like one long tracking shot, don't you think, and oh look at that bison over there, all by itself, all fenced in, perfect silhouette of its humped back against the acrylic green of the grass: seems unsure of where it stands, an escapee most probably, and this isn't where I meant to be going, but they say that wild bison live in the Wallowa Mountains, escaped from some ranch (it would appear that bison are prodigal, too). When snowstorms make the uplands impracticable, they come down the mountain to greener pastures, where some early-rising farmer is amazed to see the inimitable silhouette of one that has strayed from the herd, munching away at the grass like any old cow as it ruminates some deep memory of evasion.

The fact remains that, at the next stop, a young woman steps onto the nearly full bus and sits down right next to Perry, who at first doesn't seem to care, casting only the most cursory glance at her, not so much curious as defensive, a relic of that old animal reflex of ours that is naturally suspicious of anything that gets too close; and he went back to watching how the fields seemed stitched together under the vast skies.

While continuing to observe the landscape's seamless metamorphoses (a copse swells into a forest, which in turn shrinks away, yielding to empty prairie and the occasional farmhouse on its edge), Perry could feel the presence of the young woman next to him. The way they each went about ignoring the other (she, reading the novel she took out right after sitting down, and he, turning his face toward the window) was so conspicuous, so militantly intentional, that Perry could no longer think of anything else.

An exchange of smiles with this neighbor when she took her seat would have diminished her importance, when you thought about it, compared to this heavy silence, this mute cohabitation that caused a heightened tension between them, something electric, almost intoxicating.

Perry started imagining ways to break the ice. Still looking out the window at the continuously morphing landscape, Perry could occasionally glimpse his own face (when the background outside the glass grew darker, and his self-portrait would float, pale orange and translucent, against the dense forest). He began to come up with simple phrases, conversation-starters, an insistent look, for example, at the book she's reading, and he'd say, so what's that you're reading? Or say something about the passing views: he would turn to her, did you see that, over there, that weird building, hey look, that's a bison over there, isn't it, and he would tell her the story of the bison that fled captivity so long ago, and how they instill a certain fear in the hearts of the locals, because you probably underestimate how dangerous these big animals can be, when they get riled and charge, and Perry would keep adding layers to his story, making things up, how the older members of the herd are the grumpiest, according to scientists, and you have to wonder, Perry would add, who let them escape without alerting the authorities (if you question the ranch owners in those parts, they're all oh no, no, we're not missing a single head), since no one seems to want to own up, even though those animals are worth quite a pile of cash, that's a lot of meat just vanishing into the American wilderness. Or any object Perry would feign to suddenly need to retrieve from the pocket of his jacket that he'd stowed on the rack above the seats, since he would at the very least have to say a word of apology, sorry to bother you, and, balanced on one leg, he'd reach for the jacket, the prop that's happy to play a role in his little comedy— no harm done, right?—(the jacket is all the more willing to serve, since its master's stooped shoulders, his body language of perpetual discouragement, are hardly flattering to the cut of the coat—jackets have pride, too—and it was about time Perry got his act together, so, any way I can be of help); or, to get a better access angle to the overhead luggage rack, obliging his neighbor to get up out of her seat, and there, both of them standing, the time it takes to grab his jacket, spontaneously compare their relative heights, how well their bodies fit together, thanks, Perry would say, and she, you're welcome; now that he had his foot in the door, they could carry on, with her telling him about the novel, and him pointing through the window at trees, windmills, curiously shaped clouds.

Instead, he maintained his three-quarter turn, and she kept her eyes riveted to her novel, leisurely turning its pages, completely focused, it seemed, on that uncanny chemistry that transforms a series of print characters into story characters, into setting, into plot.

Still, he sensed that she occasionally paused to look out the window, not the one across the aisle, but Perry's window (where she could not have helped seeing his hair, an ear, the curve of his cheek), and wasn't this all in order to set up the possibility of a conversation? When she cleared her throat at one point, he couldn't help but wonder whether she was trying to get his attention, whether he should turn toward her, but since he couldn't be sure, he preferred to carry on with the imaginary conversation.

In the end, the young woman got off at the next stop, and here is what happened in Perry's heart: for the next twenty or so miles he rode without her, he felt like he missed her. The customariness of her presence that she was able to create in scarcely an hour, there was no denying it, had left a hole in his soul.

Perry made no attempt to look her up (though it would have been possible, for example, by getting off at her stop on his way back and asking around, you didn't happen to see a young woman who looks like this or that, there are so few houses around there, he'd have located her eventually). Actually, he couldn't care less whether he ever got to know her: what mattered to Perry was that this minor letdown (don't get me wrong, this wasn't just another letdown in Perry's life, but almost a fiction of a letdown, the kernel of a novel in the making), this cheap thrill, you might say, was a sign that the other one, the real, major letdown, was starting to fade into the past. The warm feeling he experienced just imagining their conversation, her unsettling physical presence as they almost touched elbows, the vacuum her departure had created, all of this amounted to a blow to Mildred's image, altering her formerly unsurpassable uniqueness, her painfully irrevocable Mildredness. And this was a really good thing. Perry had felt available, in a way, a new, welcome, unexpected availability whose effect was lifesaving.

That's what he told Harry Dean the night before he left, out in the barnyard, where Harry was getting a breath of evening air before going down to pick up Colter at the Blueberry and driving over, as always, to the *Ulysses*. At the time, Perry drew no conclusion, he just let the episode float overhead, like the cigarette smoke from Harry's last puffs, as he held the butt between thumb and index, squinting, as if he too could see the images of the young woman in the bus and of Mildred dissipating with the tar and nicotine vapor.

Also, Two or Three Things about Wendy

But let's get back to Wendy, since that's who I was talking about, when I mentioned Perry stopping by to see her before taking off into the Oregon wilderness.

Wendy, with her wrinkled face like the cracked surface of a dry creek bed, no lie, Wendy was for Colter and the others like some distant relative who'd taken them under her wing, a spinster, stiff as a board, whose unsmiling, locked-up goodness was expressed through the lavishly prepared dishes she served them (they ate like kings). Which explains why, the day I saw them for the first time at the Blueberry, they refrained from pumping their fists along with the fans in the stands, in imitation of the brawl they were watching on screen but wished they could have taken part in, preferring instead to cluck and tsk, in sympathy with Wendy, who was so appalled by the spectacle (they were like the chorus behind Wendy's solo, her admonitions louder and clearer, their notes softer and down an octave): not just to butter her up, not just so that she wouldn't skimp on their portions, but because if she, of all people, were to show them scorn, however big and manly they may have been, it would have destroyed them, because Wendy, now that everyone else, from forebears to descendants and everything in between, had blown that dump, she was all the family any of them had left.

That's why they watched their step at the Blueberry when she was around. And they got kindness in return, which was all they could aspire to. For them, Wendy was as unfathomable as an elderly aunt, the one you never dared ask to tell her story.

So brittle and austere, always obliging, but with that gravelly smoker's voice, Wendy, her parchment face that kept its past to itself, tough and efficient Wendy, monosyllabic, the girl that gets it done, that was Wendy, in a nutshell, and it didn't matter that the guys dealt with her every day, they never found out anything about her. A woman of few words, living her rigorous, Spartan life with no complaints, Wendy's was a sour solitude, a mystery that no one among the regulars at the Blueberry ever really tried to solve.

Except Harry Dean.

Harry used to say that if you managed to catch Wendy when she didn't have anything else to do, when the restaurant was empty, no one at the bar but you, and once she'd filled your mug, straightened a couple things, and made sure all was in order, she'd come out to the stoop, still in her uniform, maybe to have a cigarette (the smoke from the cigarette she held between her bony fingers rose with the same sensual swirls as anyone's), letting the gray curls dissolve into the cold air (experiencing, involuntarily, that same nostalgic effect you always feel when something is consumed before your eyes and gone forever), or to just stare out at the parking lot, and over at the road where a vehicle might be passing, and at the trees beyond that, an entire forest, and to the right, the notion of ocean, to the left, the notion of town, and between those two notions, Wendy leaning back into who knew what memory of some stillborn desire whose ghosts haunted her faded face, what vague, sorrow-ful image of her past beat painfully in her chest, calling out for release, Wendy inhaling the night air as if to dilute her demons, Harry said that was when you'd climb down from your barstool and go have your beer out by her (not seated right next to her, something in her uprightness made that impossible, but leaning on the motel sign, for example, covering up some of the letters in the process), and when that would happen, yes, Wendy might well start talking about herself.

That's how he found out (on cold afternoons, when there was nothing to do at the farm, when no crops were growing anywhere, while dormant nature was busy cooking up the season to follow) (and where was Colter then, not yet arrived in the region, or up in his room taking a nap) that Wendy had lived a long time with her mother; not only when she was growing up, but even later, coming home after work, not to an apartment of her own, which she either couldn't afford or never tried to rent, feeling responsible for her mother, just as she felt responsible for the whole world, and in particular, for the patients in her care, because, and this I haven't mentioned yet, at the time, Wendy was a nurse, so, like I said, she wouldn't be walking into her own living room and tossing her coat onto a chair before collapsing onto the sofa, but into her mother's apartment, where, every morning before going to work, she'd wash and dress her, make her tea and butter her toasts, leave her lunch in the fridge, and later in the evening, heat up a can of soup for them both, before getting her mother ready for bed; and only then would she enter her own room and shut the door on the rest of the world.

There, she'd lie down on her bed and stare at the blank ceiling, as if reading coffee grounds where she divined some future for herself, pale and neutral.

It was a flat, blank life that Wendy was leading when one day there was Tom.

There was always one, some Tom or another, to shake up your well-ordered days.

Tom turned Wendy's life into a romance novel, with expanded horizons, fresh possibilities, heightened expectations.

But the Tom novel was a short one, and Wendy ended up in a different genre, more like social realism, where your bed of roses gets mowed down.

I was listening to Harry, trying to picture what it must have been like to grow up in a little town near Portland, like the one where Wendy lived when she was living in her mother's apartment and spending her days at the clinic, slipping into her smock and clogs as soon as she entered the gray-walled corridor where their assigned lockers were located, hers among them, brave Wendy, who took care of her mother, and any other locals who needed her ministrations. Compresses, subcutaneous or intravenous shots, she could do it all (intramuscular, too), and attended to each patient with the same concern, the same concentration, each gesture precise, focused, tying the tourniquet with the same skill as she did everything else, always finding the vein on the first try, in goes the needle, you can open your fist now, she slips off the tourniquet, applies the cotton and presses, then tops it with a bandage. Wendy, irreproachable, giving herself completely over to whatever she's doing. I was listening to Harry, and thinking that's what must have set Wendy apart from the other girls who'd be chatting at their stations during a break, girls who gave the impression of standing at the confluence of endless possibilities, none of which may exist in real life, though their detailed scenarios fueled daily conversation: it's just that Wendy abstained from such reverie, living entirely in the moment, mindful of the task at hand, no more, no less.

Which is why, when Tom arrived on the scene, he modified lots of things in Wendy's heart. Not only because of the emotion his arrival infused, replacing the stalwart resignation that had defined her life until then, not only because of the nascent feelings, but because these feelings set off a myriad of "what ifs" in her head, prospects that quivered like young branches in a spring breeze.

Now, when Wendy would give you an injection, her touch was just as precise, her attention just as focused, but instead of grounding herself in the dull, unchangeable knowledge of the little apartment where she lived, instead of thinking of getting her mother fed, her mind was alive with wild imaginings that her well-behaved nature had trouble reining in, where Tom was always the featured star, the conqueror, the savior, or, why not, Tom as abuser, because when you open the door to love, you have to be ready to get knocked around.

The doomsayers of this world set traps of self-fulfilling prophecy, and Wendy was once again scrupulously determined to stick with the program and prove her mother right, as if it were more important to maintain her mother's vision as serious, trustworthy, and true than to keep her own love life alive (and how much latitude did she have, in any case?).

In this world where everything came to pass as her mother had predicted it would, Tom made promises he couldn't keep, all sorts of promises that steered Wendy's imaginings through her hectic day at the clinic, as she daydreamt about what was to come; and it all fell apart the day Tom came to tell her that he'd be moving to a distant town, a hundred miles from there, where he was going to be living with a certain Tricia, soon to be his wife.

Wendy said nothing, standing there outside the clinic, looking tiny in her overcoat that she'd just buttoned up, almost grateful that he'd come in person to let her know (lucky for you, Tom said, that I at least let you know), Wendy standing there buffeted by the storm of her collapsing love affair, but reminded almost immediately of the stable world her mother had predestined for her, with its familiar borders and landmarks, so that she might pursue her path in life as before, compliant and steady as she goes.

Which is exactly what she did, and the whole Tom episode, which could have changed her character forever (emotion and disappointment resulting in bitterness) (or on the contrary, the keen memory of exaltation whetting her appetite to try again

with someone new), seemed to disappear without a trace, the
waters finally closing over her.

Wendy, conscientious and focused before meeting Tom,
was still her same self, making what she could of her tedious
existence, the thing she knew the best.

I didn't have enough time to observe Wendy, the one time I
went to the Blueberry, but what I learned about her from Harry
confirmed my first impression. It's as if everything were already
etched into the furrows of her skin, the seriousness of her face,
that time at the Blueberry as I watched her jot down my order
on her pad, when I passed her on my way from the restroom,
brushing by her naturally, almost making contact, feeling that
vibe she was emanating (the good soldier, stalwart and depend-
able, mission-driven), before pausing a moment in front of a
glass showcase full of a sundry assortment of decorative objects,
for right there as you came out of the restroom, there was a huge
glass case filled with Elvis statuettes, made in all sizes and mate-
rials, alongside other shiny, colorful objects, metallic or plastic,
maybe some trophies, too, though I might be misremembering
that, I might be adding things that weren't there, like all the
Elvis statuettes, though I could just as well be underestimating
what the case contained—go ahead and include whatever you
want. Something about the sight of all those trinkets, combined
with the waves I was getting from Wendy's body as she passed,
enabled me to guess that she was living with her mother, unmar-
ried, curt and meticulous; even her profession, as nurse, made
sense. And her affair with Tom, a relationship that, if she ever
still thinks about it, must seem less like a lush oasis in her otherwise arid existence than a worthless episode full of energy-drain-
ing emotion: she felt no nostalgia for the man, no regrets, no
pain, this was not a happy moment she sought to reactivate in
her memory, but rather something that for a few months was
undoubtedly vital and nourished, but that, as soon as Tom was

gone, she simply freeze-dried, shrinking the memory down to a desiccated little pellet, indistinguishable from her dreary days, blending in with the rest, a deactivated thought.

Her every gesture channeled this same information, whether she was working behind the bar, or carefully jotting down your order, even though she'd been at this for years, and then taking the order slip back to the kitchen, thinking about what she was doing, fully in the moment (tear the slip from the pad along the perforation, push through the swinging doors into the kitchen, skirt the stoves to go post the order slip on the magnetic board), this high productivity that wasn't an image she was cultivating, but the truth at the core of her being, her competent, accurate, rough, naturally attentive being, who watched over Colter and Harry Dean (and Shannon, when he would show up), the way a shepherdess watches over her flock, with a benevolence that never loses sight of the irreducible otherness of the sheep species.

The First Time There Was McCain

THE TIME I'M talking about, the first time there was McCain, there was nothing particularly exciting going on right before he arrived on the scene—same old things, the humid air, the tentative confessions, and always that child in the photo, maintaining an element of mystery.

Since the issue had to be raised eventually, the question was what connected that kid to the person behind the camera. Which family member or relative was it, and how were we to figure out whether he was being protective or threatening? Or maybe both, a twofer, impossible for a child to untangle, hence the panicked look on his face: maybe that's what you saw in his eyes, attachment and fear, an absurd dependence on the person snapping the picture, from whose clutches it was impossible for the little guy to escape, because the scales of size and years tipped in the other's favor, or because blood is thicker than water, even when you're that young, you're bound to your own, think about it. That loyalty and affection in spite of (maybe) the beatings, the selfless, almost animal love that you can't help feeling toward your torturer, since he was all you knew, he'd even changed your diapers, and from the looks he gave you, you somehow knew you were his offspring. And, as if photo capture truly made captives of its snapshot subjects, that's what I was thinking that night, the child took the baited hook, the way prey does when that's all it has to grab onto for dear life.

That said, the speechless child continued to stare out at our comings and goings; and that night, when I saw McCain for the first time, "our" included Colter, Shannon, Harry Dean and me, same as always. And maybe the two truckers I mentioned earlier but haven't had a chance to say any more about, since they don't really have a role in this story, except as décor, Harper and Marvin by name, and I believe they made an appearance that night. They probably came in and did their well-rehearsed trucker thing, then left the bar early, ten minutes or so before McCain arrived.

For McCain's entrance into Moses's bar, if you've got the Fifth Symphony, Beethoven's I mean, have a listen to the first few measures. Pom pom pom pom, pom pom pom, (*G G G E-flat, F F F D*), and he slams the door behind him (the exact opposite of my first entrance there, if you recall, the lazy door that takes forever to close shut).

McCain didn't look at all familiar to me, I don't think we'd ever crossed paths in the streets of Cannon Beach; but the guys didn't treat him the way they usually treat newcomers to the bar. I got the feeling, from the way they were all suddenly on their best behavior, that McCain was right at home here.

McCain: so, imagine an overstitched beige puffer vest, an untucked wool shirt underneath, and the most salient feature, his inquisitive way of looking around, sniffing the air, making you feel like you've done something wrong, but you don't know what.

Piercing eyes beneath bushy brows, that was the look, and a furrowed forehead that formed a wavy pattern. I remember thinking just that: the blue-green of his eyes and the undulating wrinkles made McCain look like an incarnation of the ocean.

And like the ocean, he crashed into the bar like a wave, though he could also hold back in a low swell, expanding from within, a slow, contained breaker in the making, always on the verge of spilling over.

They'd see McCain maybe a couple times a year (or so said

Moses, when I asked, oh, two or three times a year, I guess), and that's all it took to remind folks he existed, though one time through would have been plenty, go figure, he wasn't the type you could forget easily.

He started out easy enough, playing the nice guy, a beer mug in one hand, served up by Moses with that same inscrutable air he'd wear in all situations. And what did McCain talk about that night? Of all things, the Irish countryside, where his ancestors came from.

He aimed his steely gaze at the three buddies or at Moses (I obviously didn't enter into the calculation), like he was searching for something, getting into their faces with his unspoken, unanswered question (some vital question, the kind you ask someone at gunpoint, making it clear that he's dead meat if he doesn't answer), and it was like all his chatter about Ireland, lakes, and megaliths, was just there to mislead, to cover his tracks. Like the Pacific over here, the Atlantic would rage unabated, eating away at the Cliffs of Moher, biting chunks out of the Aran Islands, dark and pebbly, whose fields were broken up by a network of walls. Puffins and auks wheel through the brisk air, above the seas where rorqual whale and basking shark swim. McCain was particularly keen to talk about the pectoral sandpipers and the northern gannets that soar over ruins and dunes, but you got the impression that meant something else entirely. He went on about stinging sea anemones, green shore crabs, greater white-fronted geese, and short-eared owl, he described bloody cranesbill and the peatlands, blackface sheep and Connemara ponies, kestrel falcons and heather-bell, and it all came across like nothing but threats and intimidation.

The more he talked about fly-fishing, whitewater and rushing streams, the more details he gave about waterfalls and granite boulders, the tenser we felt, an inexplicable tension that had nothing to do with what he was saying.

McCain certainly came from around here. He must have been heir to some story that left a huge impression on the locals, something his father passed down, or on the contrary, as a fatherless child, he told a tale that brought a tear to the eye. It was on such tearful stories that McCain slowly built his empire, the enfant terrible whose wish was your command, who was still getting everything he asked for, even today.

I watched him as he continued to rave about the dolmens and the craggy inlets, the arid uplands and the jagged coastline, the giant ferns and drippy grottos, green valleys and fjords, pebbly beaches and greater celandine poppies, and all I could think was that he'd come to stake out his territory.

I had no way to prove my hunch, but it seemed to me that this whole number he was doing about Ireland, when it was so obvious that something else was at issue, was somehow aimed right at me. He was trying to give me a lesson, encoded, mysterious and discontinuous, but a lesson nonetheless, whose message became crystal clear: I had no business being here.

Later on, once McCain had left, since he did eventually leave, satisfied for the time being that I'd got the message, the encrypted threat beneath his rant on Ireland's savage beauty, I found out that he lived up in the hills, and that, as far as he was concerned, everything he could see from his house belonged to him. And that included Cannon Beach, which spread out below him like a scale model, with the tiny *Ulysses*, the motel, and the houses in between.

McCain spent his days up there in his house, ruminating over his dominion, based on I'm not quite sure what. Enjoying the vast overlook his position afforded, the view his eyes embraced, as if holding something in one's gaze signified possession of it.

The three buddies must have found something distressing about McCain's mythical Ireland number, since they left the bar as soon as he'd finished. Moses closed up a little earlier than usual, and I sat out on the stoop for a long while afterward, trying to sober up in the night wind.

All was quiet, the dogs were asleep, even the ocean lay low. I was trying to reorganize my thoughts. As I sat there on the wooden step, it felt as if they were scattered at my feet, that I had to gather them up one by one. And put them back in the right order.

Maybe McCain caught sight of me once through his binoculars, as he stood at his picture window and panned across the streets of Cannon Beach in close-up, and hold on there, wait a second, who the hell's that guy, frowning at the presence of an outsider, whom he probably went on to sight on other occasions, keeping an eye on my movements, between the windswept beach, the motel, and Moses's bar.

Because here's what happened since that night at the bar, I began to obsess over McCain. I plotted out a whole storyline, imagining his house up there, his lookout post for overseeing the entire town. I saw it all, the one-story ranch-style house, the picture windows that reflected the trees from outside (he had a few right in his yard), and through which McCain kept watch on everyone, hunkered down in his living room, zooming in and out with his long lens, watching Mary enter the grocery store where she worked, Shannon right behind her, Tim opening the door to the tourist shop, and then coming up against my silhouette, he's been here a little too long for my liking, would grumble McCain, who could then saunter down into town whenever he felt like it and resolve the anomaly (some French guy who's getting a little too comfortable here, that's an anomaly if I've ever seen one, in McCain's opinion), just to make sure everybody knows who's boss in Cannon Beach, where everything seemed peaceful, mired in the toneless tedium of an empty seaside resort in the off-season (which amounts to three out of four). But it was his, and he reigned supreme with an uncontested authority that had to come from somewhere, but the hell if I knew where.

Sure, he might well come down to town because he's just bored, and then, McCain would tell his henchmen (because he had to have henchmen, right?) to keep an eye on things but not to wait up, he was going out tonight (bring one gorilla along, though, to follow at a certain distance, a kind of bodyguard, just in case; that one must have been standing just outside the door on the night we got lectured on the splendors of the Emerald Isle), and maybe he happened upon me there at the bar entirely by chance—no big deal, right?—and spent the evening talking to the guys he'd known for years, paying no attention at all to my presence, apart from giving me the vague impression that I was a non-entity.

Well, maybe, I thought, gathering my wits as best I could, trying to tame the uncanny fear that had gripped me back in the bar as soon as I saw McCain burst through the door with a cockiness that meant nothing but trouble. Maybe it was all just a gigantic coincidence. But it could also be (fear's getting the better of me again, or is it just caution) that he really did come down to issue me a warning, knowing what would happen later (and it's the *later* that I'm getting at here) if I didn't take him seriously.

Still sitting there on the stoop, I didn't know which version to believe. I was really starting to feel the cold on my face, like getting slapped by the wind. The sky was deep and dark, and there was no moon to shed light on all this.

Pliny's Uncle

I CAN'T TELL whether it was that first visit by McCain that set it all in motion, or whether things had been germinating for a while without my noticing.

What's certain is that there were episodes that should have raised a red flag, things I just let pass at the time, that take on a whole other meaning when I think about them now.

Trivial things at first, small annoyances, stuff I started wondering about.

For example, that story that Moses told me.

On the Mount St. Helens event, I did a little homework and found out it was what's known as a Plinian eruption. I'm not just trying to sound smart when I say this, but you'll see later that the term assumes a special meaning. It's called by that name in memory of the ancient Roman, Pliny the Younger, whose description of the eruption of Vesuvius set the standard and coined the term, especially regarding the ash plume that characterizes this kind of violent volcanic eruption.

And here's my point: Pliny also, during the eruption, had a story involving an uncle.

Several weeks after Moses told me the story, I went to the tiny public library adjacent to the grocery store. Picture a single room, wall-to-wall shelving, in the middle of which sits an individual wearing a puffer jacket (the place was poorly heated) and thick glasses, mouth gaping, as if he'd finally given up trying to breathe through the nose. A three-in-one hole, good for eating, talking and breathing. I say "talk," but I never got more than a few grunts out of the guy, words that his syllable-chewing diction had ground to a pulp before they got anywhere near his lips, and that came out all panting, groggy and deformed, when they weren't dead on arrival.

I looked through the stacks for the letter P, and found that, for whatever unfathomable reason, they had a copy of Pliny's *Letters*. The only person who had ever checked it out (for now, I'll stick to the facts) was Moses, whose clunky penmanship, if you ask me—limping upstrokes and twisted downstrokes— produced a clumsily legible signature on the card at the back of the book.

The volume is still on my nightstand, next to the two Lewis and Clark tomes that Harry gave me. I never got the chance to return it.

If you read it, on that very ancient day that Vesuvius spewed its famous plume into the Latin sky, Pliny was in Misenum.

Here's how it went.

The ground has been trembling for a while, but no one is overly worried, since small-scale quakes are common in the region. Then one night, the quakes become more intense. Pliny and his mother, jolted awake, take refuge in their interior courtyard. No way of knowing whether they were in total darkness, or whether there was a moon that night to light this scene of mother and son cowering, fearfully awaiting disaster.

On the other side of the wall is the sea, whose languid waves they could probably hear. The sea knew itself to be mobile, and the ground to be stable. But tonight, the world is out of kilter, with the earth moving in waves and the sea in panicked retreat, as if fleeing the spectacle, leaving fish to die in its wake in the inadequate air of the beach.

At dawn, Pliny and his mother, like many other locals, decide to leave the unsteady village that is threatening collapse at any moment. But hardly have they reached the surrounding countryside than an unreal darkness veils the earth. Pliny is dragging his mother forward by the hand, she's tripping

and falling, but he urges her on. Go without me, she tries to
persuade him, your life is more important than mine. Not
without you, mother, my life is nothing if I leave yours behind,
and they keep moving, mother and son, the mother moaning
that she's slowing them down, but he is relentless, as the rain of
ash catches up with them bit by bit.

Soon, they can see nothing at all. People call out to one
another and grope in the gloom, darkness at noon. Mother and
son are still joined, son clutching his mother's hand, by now red
and bruised by her son's ruthless grip, mother and son staunchly
linked in this archetypal pose.

And still, the ash continues to rain down, thickening the
air. It is impossible to go any further. They sit down and wait,
however they can manage, standing to brush themselves off
every so often so as not to be buried alive.

And on and on, standing, brushing, sitting, and still, the
ash.

And the uncle in all this?

The narrative is unclear in this regard. You get the feeling
that Pliny would have liked his uncle to act heroically. But
between you and me, he looks more like a braggart, this uncle
of his, all bluster and show.

While Pliny and his mother are huddled together in fear,
suffocating in the toxic, ash-laden air, the uncle is on the other
side of the bay.

As recently as the previous day, he'd been at their home.
In late afternoon, he was reading after his bath when his sister
comes to tell him that an odd-looking cloud is rising in the sky.
And presto, here's our uncle up in a flash, lacing his sandals and
out the door. He climbs a promontory and sees it's coming from
Vesuvius. No matter, thinks the uncle, but let's go get a closer
look. He finds a boat and rows toward the danger, dazzled by
the otherworldly beauty of the cloud, thrilling at this omen of
catastrophe. But the spray of stones is slowing him down, as is

the freakish retreat of the sea, which I alluded to earlier. Enough
of this, thinks the uncle, let's head over to Pomponianus's place
and wait it out; once there, he makes it sound as if there were
nothing to worry about, with a pretentiousness appreciated
only by his nephew (who may well have made some of this
up, but who enthusiastically describes his uncle as courageous,
high-spirited, and relaxed, the flip side of which, in my view, is
an annoying penchant for bravado—I'm just calling it as I see
it—and self-aggrandizement). Pomponianus (I didn't make that
name up) is completely puzzled by this clown who is making
light of the fact that a nearby volcano is spewing weird stuff.
The uncle then proceeds to bed and gets a good night's rest.
Pliny makes a point of saying that his uncle experienced no
anxious sleeplessness or worry-induced dreaming, but slept like
a log. Who knows, that may well have been, but eventually, the
noise from rocks falling on the roof wakes him, and he gets up.
And so it was that, in the middle of the night, Pomponianus
and the others leave the house as it shakes above the quaking
earth. Before leaving, they all fashion hats out of pillows and
wear them to protect their heads from flying rocks; and on they
go, a motley brigade in their feather-stuffed cotton helmets
under an angry sky.

The sun rose the next day but light could not penetrate the ash
that still hung in the air. The silhouetted figures, pillows tied
to their skulls, continued their trek through the dim morning.

Tragedy ensued.

Pliny's uncle didn't come out of it as well as did Moses's.

Pliny's uncle, also named Pliny, is linked to his nephew by
name but also by the pleasure they both derived from writing.

The nephew's quill hovers over the page. How do you describe
that enormous, puffy plume forming above the volcano? A thing
that flashed in their retinas, that they were seeing for the first
time ever, stunningly novel. The young man looks around his
study, groping for the right words, some equivalent, a familiar

object that would help readers visualize the phenomenon. He
dips his quill into the ink, wondering how to describe the
unspeakable. His gaze wanders out the window and falls upon
a stone pine. Wait, isn't that exactly the shape I'm looking for,
the way it splays at the top, branches into layers and goes frothy
at the top. And that's how that peaceful shade tree, the perfect
spot to take a nap, came to describe the splendid horror of a
column of ash. Like a stone pine, the nephew writes out in
his elegant calligraphy, and the simile helps him overcome the
lingering grief. For the uncle (still wearing the pillow on his
head?) goes over to dip a toe in the water: the sea is unnavigable,
he pronounces, and with that, they all renounce escaping by
boat. The air above the beach is thicker than ever. The uncle
stands there, his lungs breathing in the stifling vapor. The toxic
gasses were what did him in.

The uncle falls to the ground, asphyxiated, unbeknownst to
the nephew and his mother, who, at this point, know nothing of
the uncle's whereabouts, as they sit beneath the endless shower
of ash that is covering everything, like a blanket of freshly-fallen
snow.

Did Moses get this far in his reading?

Had someone told him, hey, you should go read Pliny the
Younger, and you'll see that there's someone else with an uncle
who ran out as soon as he saw the plume rising, and kept running
right at an erupting volcano? And Moses, did he dive right into
the part that interested him and, while discovering a certain
commonality, conclude that he was luckier than Pliny, since his
uncle, who everyone in the family was sure had perished in the
poisonous fumes, had eventually gotten in touch to say he was
alive, a few months later, brutally relieving them of their burden
of mourning?

Or something else that's been nagging me, did Moses make
the whole thing up? His story, told to me in confidence, a gift

he'd never given to Colter or the others, was it all bogus?

Maybe the reason Moses kept so quiet behind his bar was that, as soon as he opened his mouth, his imagination would get the best of him, he couldn't help it. A general propensity of his that I shouldn't feel offended by. But if he did fabricate the whole story, wasn't it with the intention of bamboozling me personally, me the Frenchie, solemnly, maliciously sitting me down at a back table to tell me what is now looking like a highly suspicious fairytale of his own making (let's see, what could I tell him that would be really dramatic), not so hard to come up with, since just a few days before, let's say, taking an interest in volcanoes, since he'd spent all his life right next to one, he went to the little library and took out the Pliny volume, read the pertinent pages, up there in the room where the previous summer's flypaper strips were still dangling from the ceiling?

I was really starting to wonder, the day I read the story of Pliny's uncle and then went to Moses's place. I watched him as he worked, on the other side of the counter, where he'd resumed his impenetrable air, and no one could have guessed that we'd had this heart-to-heart, that night when I was the only one in the bar, when Moses launched into his grand narrative. He had retreated into the fortress of his body, behind its impregnable walls, where not even I was now sure what he was hiding. I sat for a long time out on the stoop after closing time, smoking and revisiting all that in my head. It was the same deep, dark sky, the same barking dogs, the same distant groan of the waves. Holding my cigarette butt between thumb and index, I flicked it, just like that, right into a puddle, where bacteria were thriving unhindered, with the gorgeous night all to themselves.

Ping-Pong

I'LL BET McCAIN's henchmen (let's not lose sight of them) can sometimes be heard playing ping-pong on the little patio behind the house.

Their bling bracelets swing with each twist of wrist, the balls make their signature *pock* sound on the table, a sound like no other, light and hollow, a little like the pop sound you make with a finger inside a cheek to imitate the uncorking of champagne, that's the closest to it, though a bit more crystalline, maybe.

The uneven rhythm suggests long and short shots, lobs and slams or whatnot. *Pock* goes the ball off the rubberized roughness of the paddle, and here comes a slice, and there goes some topspin, while you're at it, a kind of brushing movement, if you will, best way to return a slice, to which you should counter with more topspin (just some friendly advice), and on it goes on McCain's patio, with the ocean churning below, a bluish-gray visible through the pines.

They go through all the strokes, from forehand pushes to backhand sidespin serves, those especially, jumping back and forth on the concrete, inhaling the iodine-infused air rising from below.

Here's a pretty harmless backhand, followed by the smash it deserves. And when they're really on their game, they bring out the sidespin, throwing the opponent off his guard.

Because that's the real benefit of playing ping-pong out in the sea breeze, the wins, the personal satisfaction gained, the short-lived revenge they get against one another, shifting their interpersonal conflicts to the tabletop, defusing the petty jealousies that would otherwise poison the atmosphere; unless it were just the opposite, fueling their frustrations, feeding their simmering feuds, adding dishonor to dishonor, it could also work like that, while McCain, lying in his hammock behind the picture window, likes to see them taking it out on each other so that they can forget him for a while, the real boss, the authority figure, adulated and despised, as are all godfathers, and solitary, yes, despite their constant presence, he's the brains of the business, the one who does the math, who thinks things through, makes all their decisions for them. And sometimes, in his heart of hearts, assuming he has one (and he necessarily does), he must yearn for stasis, a bit of peaceful laziness, yearn to just let go, if only letting go were even an option.

But laziness and tranquility are not in the cards for McCain, only vigilance. Because the pop of the ping-pong ball, that sharp little *pock* I referred to, sounds to McCain like idleness, his men's boredom resounding in the hollowness of the ball, delivered from one side of the net to the other, boredom suspended a few milliseconds in the air, then smashed by the other side, slammed across the table with the full force of the wooden paddle, pushed and driven, while McCain (from his hammock, as I said, but sometimes from his deep leather couch) plots his next move, or at least pretends to be plotting, making sure his men think that's what he's doing, devising schemes for them to execute upon his orders, these men who are both protected and hamstrung by their boss's intelligence, who will occasionally rebel, though they wouldn't call it that, caught up in the torment of their unspoken revolt that clashes with their equally strong sense of indebtedness, since he's the one who plucked them all off the street and turned them into something, into a family—in other words, what makes them grateful is also what they find so stifling.

Whether lounging in the soft fabric of his hammock or on his large throw pillows, or even standing at the big picture window looking down on the little toy village through the few conifers growing in his yard, McCain must brood dimly over the patio and those endless ping-pong matches, about all the other rooms as well where his men spread out and try to keep busy, some playing cards, the old-fashioned way, others playing point-and-shoot games on their laptops, blasting everything that moves in their pixelated on-screen universe where they imagine themselves springing into action, giving chase, bumping off one guy after the next, with only their eyes and fingers in motion (and probably some neurons up there under the scalp), temporarily exterminating tanks, soldiers, or sci-fi creatures, as well as their own caustic thoughts that fuel the urge to revolt. And the thought of this equivocal presence in his home, undisciplined and armed, scattered throughout the house, McCain realizes that danger can come from both outside (isn't that why they're there, to protect him from it, poised to act at the slightest alert, and he knows he can count on them to get him out of any brawl) and from within. Which is why he has to provide them with a mission every so often, to remind them who's calling the shots, to renew their pride in serving some purpose, happy to be marching to his orders (their big boss, so proactive and forward-thinking), they who, when they have no assignment and are just hanging around McCain's house, will sometimes begin to feel like beetles flipped onto their backs, legs flailing wildly, unable to flip back over.

McCain senses his men's mounting restlessness, and knows that at some point, it will prove more than he can handle. And maybe one day, he'll be found stabbed to death in his chair—I'm being blunt here—no trace of the perpetrator, his minions having fled, scattering into the forest, or more likely, up to Portland, where it'll be easier to disappear in the crowd. And there, they will each seek a new life, a fresh start, not as racy, certainly, but each will be his own boss, and that will change them, all that freedom, all that initiative-taking, all that choice.

Behind the picture window, it's begun to dawn on McCain that he, like all powerful men, will go into decline, before eventually being knocked off by one of his own, maybe even his number one, the Brutus complex that lurks in the heart of every favorite.

Pock, pock, pock go the ping-pong balls, each bounce underscores the henchmen's boredom, hammers it in. And this percussive beat of boredom reaches McCain's ears that decipher, with a hint of fear and a deep-seated fatalism, this Morse message sent by his men.

Paradise Lost (Shannon's Story)

STILL OTHER MOMENTS should have triggered the alarm. But it was as if I'd inadvertently switched off the system, cut the current and then gone about my business, carefree, between the motel and the bar, and that dubious ocean whose thrashing waves should have provided my first clue as to what loomed ahead. Here's one for you, for instance: the time I ran into Shannon, in daylight hours for once, on my way to the grocery store where Mary worked.

Seeing him like that, without the other guys, in the light of day (sober, worried-looking and white as a sheet, frowning sternly), he seemed like another man altogether. He must have been thinking the same thing about me, because instead of crossing the street, shaking hands and suggesting we go get a drink someplace where we could sit and talk, all he did was flash the slightest hint of a grin from the opposite sidewalk (he probably meant it as a smile, but the most restrained of smiles, corners of the mouth barely lifting at all), with a sudden glint of the eye that said he recognized who I was.

It must have been the wrong place and the wrong time, or even the wrong light: we'd meet again some other time, is what I concluded from the encounter, and shrugged off the snub before it had a chance to rile me (because we all know how that kind of feeling can blow out of proportion, if you let it). Caught up as I was in the day-to-day happenings of Cannon Beach, this scene seemed harmless enough at the time. I can see now that I should have taken it more seriously. Something about the nasty pallor of Shannon's face should have tipped me off, the cold hostility in that gaze, so turned in on its own thoughts. He kept walking, zipped into that blue puffer jacket of his, looking a paler blue than usual under the spray of whitish photons released from the chalky sky.

Shannon also had a story that he kept inside like a dead weight, but unlike Colter, never felt like telling anyone. Bits and pieces would slip, when he was too drunk to hold them back. When that happened, it was like the story was forcing its way out, exiting the mouth like a tapeworm. Chunks of the story would spill onto the bar, night after night, and in no particular order, which we would then attempt to assemble, accepting that there might be some pieces missing—because there are always pieces missing.

It was a dark, nebulous story that his alcohol-soaked mind and slurred diction made even more obscure. It seems to have all centered on the *Paradise Lost*, a private nightclub. Way out in the middle of some fir trees, it opened only certain nights, never the same ones (you had to know someone to find out), and local bands would play there, God knows where someone dug them up, from basements or attics where they hung out the rest of the time, because their weird goth personae weren't something you saw every day around here, where everyone was either a farmer, a gas station attendant, or a motel clerk in an otherwise vacant land.

When these guys got on stage, it was all metal piercings and studs, long black overcoats they threw off when it got too hot in the place, revealing torn T-shirts that showed their ghastly white torsos. And when they opened their mouths, you wondered how they ever got the notion that they knew how to sing, or how the guitarist had the nerve to blast out his chords in public, same for the drummer; it was so obvious that they should have just stayed in their garage, hopefully with lots of acoustic insulation, and rocked their brains out in private. But they were local boys, after all, the pride of Oregon, so they bellowed their hate-filled lyrics and wailed the manifesto of their violent, ephemeral philosophy into inadequately adjusted mikes that produced ear-splitting feedback, to top it off.

How did Shannon end up in a dive like that, in his same old puffer jacket and polar fleece? What possessed him to go prowling around that backwoods place?

He'd been wandering through the fir trees until he found himself within a short distance of the *Paradise*, and every time he told the story, he began with the deep, dark woods, twisted trees and evil thorny bushes that tore at your clothes as you passed.

A hostile place, like it was alive or something, Shannon said, gesticulating. You'd have sworn the thorns were grabbing at you on purpose, like the woods were out to get you. Tree roots tripped you, causing you to fall as you cursed and swore in the darkness: and down he'd go, onto the pine needles and dry leaves, his clothes now covered in decaying vegetation. Come on, get up, don't just lie there facedown in the dirt where all kinds of critters can get at you. But when he got up, scraping his hands in the process, he just missed hitting his head on an overhead branch, which triggered another string of expletives as he raged against the trickster night. So there was Shannon, inching his way through the vast forest, bruised and battered, clothes tattered, brutalized by the great outdoors.

In that same forest, whenever I heard him get all resentful about how the woods had tripped him up that night when he set out to do who knows what instead of going home to Mary and his little apartment, after leaving Moses's place, heading up the main street (the others all rode home in the pickup), and then, for whatever reason, forking into the dark pines, in that same forest, a century earlier, the men of the Lewis and Clark expedition had slogged through the same woodlands, and when Shannon described how he had to fight his way through the thorny underbrush, I imagined they had learned how to negotiate the bumps and dips, to outsmart the tree roots that rose like swollen veins, because trees don't grow only upward, but outward as well, in all directions, invasive root systems that spread far and wide, grazing the ground with their long, knotty fingers, crooked, arthritic and weird.

In some places, the roots protruded so high they could sit in them. They formed low hollows, seats where they could squat for a moment, legs tucked to their chest, cricket-like, a tentative woodland respite, a little uncomfortable, and it was then the men would be assailed by doubt, as they were each time the body allowed itself any reprieve from physical demands, and notions would rush in to occupy the void, as the memory of those they'd left behind on the other side of the continent flickered in their minds, all the questions relating to the return trip, to its very possibility.

They would then get themselves up, guns slung over their shoulders, and continue hunting among the now desiccated, friable ferns. Not those tender, supple, newly-unfurled fiddleheads, but ragged, crispy underbrush that crunched annoyingly underfoot, alerting the fowl and small game, which would skedaddle even before the men could cock their weapons.

So, it was in this hunter's nightmare of noisy undergrowth that they pressed on. It crackled, caught on their clothing, where it left little rust-colored spores. They came back to camp empty-handed, and attempted to shed what clung to their trousers, in great sweeping motions, palms to fabric, ranting and cussing: didn't everything seem to be conspiring against them?

But Shannon wasn't thinking about them that night. Trees got in his way, and invisible creeping creatures were poised to spring from the thickets, muffled in the gloom until the moment of attack.

Shannon was on the lookout, alone in the woods, heart thumping.

How long did this wary trek last, as hostile, brutal nature closed in with every step, scraping and scratching him as he crunched his way across the forest floor, until some creature leapt out at him, in the form of man or beast—we couldn't tell from his incoherent narrative: was it a wild boar, a bear, a rapist—striking under cover of night?

He couldn't see a thing, but he should have been able to tell if it was human by the breathing, by how it was panting from the effort. Or by how it felt (stiff-bristled or whatnot), how tall it was, how big.

How come he couldn't answer when we asked, when he started telling the story in spite of himself, when Colter would shake him up and ask what the hell he was talking about, what was it, the damn thing that attacked you, but Shannon, he just kept it all very vague and jumbled, not caring whether it made any sense: his words came at you like fists in a free-for-all, and we ended up knowing little more than this: a scary night walk in the woods where someone or something jumped him.

So what really happened during that nocturnal tussle among the pines, atop that bed of needles thick on the ground?

Was Shannon really the victim, or might he have been the aggressor? Because the question necessarily keeps coming back as to what he was doing in the immediate environs of the *Paradise Lost*.

Could it be that he'd decided (and this sounds like classic Shannon) that he was going to go teach them a lesson, those punks at the *Paradise*, to go rough up some kid that might be hanging around outside after one of the sets, just as plastered as he was, some scrawny weakling who'd go down after a few punches? Is that the notion he got into his head when he left the main road and headed into the wooded hills, was he spoiling for a fight, was there some rage he had to take out on someone before heading home?

He would always stop the narrative at the same place: the night trek through the woods, the fear, constant alert, and finally the attack, the anonymous body coming down on his, rolling on the ground with him, and that's where he'd stop. Was he ashamed to take the story any further?

How far did it go, this *mano a mano* on a moonless night, each groping sightlessly, a sylvan battle of the blind, with only touch, smell and hearing to sense where the other was at any moment? With the pines standing by, non-participatory, silent and unshakable, frozen in their robes and pointy hoods, like Ku Klux Klansmen (the comparison just occurred to me), and was it his own failure, his coming out of it as loser, getting the crap beat out of him without landing a single punch of his own, is that what was torturing Shannon? The other guy's physical superiority, out there in the woods with only the trees to bear witness, or was it just the reverse? How badly did he mess up the other guy?

Other questions were also raised, and in particular, whether Shannon just happened to be over by the *Paradise* that night, or instead, whether he knew one of the young guys who hung out at the club.

There were those, Colter in particular, who thought that Shannon had a son (there was a rumor going around), and I don't mean the sons he had from his first marriage with the woman he ended up leaving with their four children, who continued to grow a little every day, with their boyhood problems, toys, book bags, and insects to dismember; no, I'm talking here about a son he is thought to have sired when he was much younger, somewhere in the region, since Shannon did used to live here, at first, before leaving for somewhere else and starting the little family I just mentioned, and then evacuating that situation to go live with Mary in their two-room place by the ocean, not so much fleeing as returning, you might say.

This first son, at the start, it's believed that he checked in on him, calling the mother sporadically, from a phone booth, trying to get up the courage but not finding words to match what he was feeling, what he wanted to say about the son, because what did he want, what would anyone want when you suddenly have a son with a woman you know next to nothing about, except that you had no intention of living with her, and who gets up on her high single-mother horse and starts hurling abuse at you as soon as she recognizes your voice at the other end of the line? Her insults crackled into the receiver (there used to be receivers back then) while he stared at the pedestrian traffic through the dirty glass of the booth, people passing by as if nothing were happening behind the opaline partition, separated from him not only by the glass and the layer of grime that gave everything outside a hazy, matte finish, but by the difference in emotions they were experiencing: there he was, trying to extricate himself from a real-time confrontation with this vituperating voice, but no one anywhere bothered to listen to his side of the story, least of all her, who had already made up her mind about the kind of person he was, without caring whether her version bore any resemblance to the facts of the case: it was her story and she was sticking to it, no matter how much damage she was causing everyone, herself included, as she turned it all over and over in her heart, and in Shannon's, with her destructive rage. Still holding the receiver, Shannon truly felt that everything she was accusing him of had nothing to do with him, but he didn't know how to put that into words, so he just stood there, her false accusations on the one hand, his denial and indecisiveness on the other, and the neutral position of the people outside the glass booth, still performing their walk-on role in this drama, without so much as a glance in his direction. And as she was screaming at him to never phone her again, he could hear the kid in the background, the voice of his own child, starting to wail.

Then one day, a teenager by then, and Shannon having given up trying to make contact, unable to even find out where the mother was living since they moved in with the now step-father who was taking up more and more room in this dysfunctional three-person household, the boy left home. How Shannon found out about his son running away, I have no idea, but he was haunted by it ever since, the idea that his son was scraping by somewhere in the region, hiding out, that he might be living rough, in the woods all by himself, or maybe with a group, in some basement, or an attic or garage, with nothing but a sleeping bag to his name, getting high on whatever he could lay his hands on, wondering about his real father, the way Shannon wondered about him. He probably burned with feelings of abandonment, a fire the mother had most certainly stoked, even though things were much more complicated than that. But sons tend to oversimplify.

So if what folks at Cannon Beach were whispering was true, the story of the first son that Shannon would refer to obliquely before retreating into silence, then it wasn't beyond the realm of possibility that one night, on his way home from the bar, he got the notion into his head that his son might be up at the *Paradise*.

One night, when he was brooding again over his son's disappearance while the others were talking noisily around him at the bar, and when, once he'd stumbled outside into the crisp air, and was hit by a sudden gust of wind, it came to him like an illumination that he had to go have a look at the *Paradise*.

Or maybe some locals had clued him in (as a kind of favor, but then you know how vicious people can be, slipping in a word or two they know will be hurtful, for no particular reason—

go figure what lurks in the hearts of men) that they thought they might have seen his son hanging around the *Paradise*. At that, his heart must have skipped a beat, and without thinking twice, he set his mind on going to the club, finding the kid and beating the bejesus out of him, not even really knowing why, just the idea that a father's place is to lay down the law, and that place had been vacant for a long time. Just for the physical contact with his son, even if it meant confrontation, even without understanding that it was really about how much he loved the boy.

Maybe that was it, the repressed story he kept returning to without ever getting to the nub. Not the kind of story you want to be telling other people, your kid hanging out with the *Paradise Lost* crowd. Anyway, they already knew about the kid, that wasn't the problem, but there was something taboo in the region about the *Paradise Lost*, a place that had appeared like a malignant growth on the territory, planted there among the pines like an evil curse.

If Colter, Harry, and Shannon had ever felt the urge to go rough up some poor suckers just for the heck of it—and their buddies from the *Ulysses* would have certainly come along for the fun—it's pretty likely they'd have headed for the *Paradise*. Just as you could easily imagine the *Paradise* bunch deciding to make a little side trip down to the *Ulysses*, down to the coast *en masse*, a Goth army descending on the town to dethrone the fathers, the older generation, those who'd accepted squalor as their natural habitat, and insignificance as their lot in life, where the Goths, in their long coats that opened like wings in the ocean breeze, believed they had chosen revolt.

It's possible that things got pretty nasty with the son (even though I'd rather not think about it) that night in the dark forest, because, for one thing, they weren't competing in the same category, Shannon weighing in at well over 200 pounds, the clear heavyweight of the two, and the super-featherweight son barely clearing 130.

It's also possible that Shannon went there only to see his son, and that on the way, he was attacked by someone else. A total stranger, maybe on acid, who didn't know what he was doing, why he was jumping on some random guy, just because of shoes crunching on dry leaves, because of someone's heavy breathing and the frightening proximity of another body in the solitude of pitch-dark timberland.

And Shannon, tanked as he was, but still stronger than his younger assailant, must have flattened him, but how badly, that's the question. The other guy was maybe breathing his last on the forest floor while Shannon, somehow managing to get himself vertical, panting like an ox in the deserted darkness (he didn't call for help, don't even bother asking), made his way back down to Cannon Beach (the wind off the ocean dried the blood on his face, while the first light of day was bringing the landscape back into view), with thoughts punching so hard that they cancelled each other out.

I wonder whether even Shannon knew for sure. Can you recognize your son merely by the heat his body gives off, or the way he breathes as he walks up to punch you in the face?

The Tillamook Lighthouse

IT COMES BACK sometimes, that seagull from a while ago when I first got here, making another attempt at occupying my guardrail, wondering if this might be a good perch for feeding, craning to look inside my room to check whether the occupant might have changed, if that snooty, uncaring Frenchman is still there, the one it tried to make friends with, against all odds, or has he been replaced by a more understanding, considerate person. And seeing that it's the same old guy, it persists anyway, I'm the one it will have to soften, to convince, whose attitude it needs to adjust. It knows it's me, yet it believes in the persuasive powers of its cute little neck movements, its sideways glances, its little dance steps, on one leg, then the other, on the iron rail outside my room, a circus act performed against the background of an increasingly cloudy sky.

These birds learn from prior experience with motel regulars who are so happy to see them when they take up quarters again in their old vacation spot (they've hardly put their bags down than the gulls fly in to greet them, or so they believe) that they're tossing them bits of bacon from the very first meal they cook with a joy bordering on affection (and I'll bet that when they're not vacationing at Cannon Beach, they tell everyone back home about these winged visitors, as they sit in their living rooms, remembering the fun they had with the gulls (you should see them, they're so graceful, and smart as all get-out), really missing them). This particular gull is proud to list all the new vacationers it's performed for, reprising the same song-and-dance routine that wins them over every time, knowing that its little soft-shoe sidestep will earn it whatever it wants.

As for me, no thanks, I don't want anything to do with any seagull. You won't catch me exchanging loving glances with it, or projecting a personality on the damn thing, or worse, waiting around every day for it to show up. Nope, no way.

I'd rather watch the rain.

The way it batters the waves.

Full-throttle, unsurpassable rain that pours down onto the ocean, as if it knew where it came from.

It pummels the breakers with the same unprovoked anger, or even violence sometimes, alas, that we express against our forebears just to prove our uniqueness, a head-on confrontation, because sometimes, it's the only way to construct one's selfhood. And at the same time, it's coming home, the prodigal rain that had evaporated, left for good, and now is dragging itself back, however it can, all bluster and swagger, nothing subtle about him, teenage rain, if you will; and the ocean opens its arms and accepts—or not: when it swallows it whole, opening its massive jaws, furious ogre that refuses to forgive its progeny for escaping its clutches, when it absorbs it, shuts the door and calls it a day, teaching the runaway rain a good lesson.

Sometimes, I force myself to get up, take the few steps between my bed and the window. I stand as steady as I can, the horizon at about eye level, and I follow the line from left to right, until I see the Tillamook Lighthouse.

Tillamook Rock Lighthouse, rising out of its basalt foundation, occasionally completely fogged in, but usually a solitary land-mark, in sharp focus, a slender finger scratching the sky.

Fog banks make their daily attempt to erase it from the scenery, prevailing winds batter it relentlessly, storms do their best to topple it; but each time, it reappears, stoic yet wounded.

Windows inevitably break, flooding is frequent, rock fragments
hurled by the waves cause structural damage, it's happened (and
the foghorn doesn't work anymore). You could hardly think of
a worse spot, but that's why it's there, because there are storms
and high waves, craggy, sharp-edged rocks. Or at least, that's
why it was there, since it's out of service now (Oswald Allik
was the name of the last lighthouse keeper—picture him in his
sou'wester, too tight in the arms for his bulky sweaters, braving
the elements and the solitude, at the foot of the lighthouse, hands
in pockets, looking out at that nasty ocean that's snapping at his
heels like a mean old dog. Oswald alone with his thoughts, in
that dark, damp tower, climbing up and back down, what else
is there to do, fixing the same old things that keep breaking,
Oswald could take up a whole novel all by himself).

As it stands, I don't know, sometimes I think that maybe Shannon's son has been hiding out in the belly of that lighthouse
after all. I'm talking about the first son, the one he had with the
young woman who used to insult him over the phone whenever
he called, and who's probably the reason why he left the region
in the first place, before coming back after he realized that the
little family he'd created somewhere else was a bust (the kids who
did nothing but fight, totally ignoring him, the wife who gave
him the cold shoulder, an unlivable situation of hostile coexis-
tence), and moving in with Mary, who welcomed him into her.
      This son, one night, deciding to flee his mother's toxic
harangues that filled their tiny apartment (nothing but
cursing and berating, from atop her lofty perch of matriarchal
superiority), just as he was also fleeing the stepfather whose
dubiously passive presence was the main ingredient of their
contentious relationship, left the apartment and disappeared
into the forest, and maybe found an old skiff of some kind,
and rowed himself out to the lighthouse. And there he'd be,
listening all day to the waves crashing onto the rocks, and at

night, watching the mirrored reflection of waning moons off the foamy crests of the waves until it made him seasick.

The son always on the lookout, quivering, never at ease. The son missing a father whose face he's never seen. And sometimes, as he gazes into the speckled mirror still hanging over the sink in the lighthouse, he imagines he sees his father back when he conceived him. About the same age, he thinks, the same air of indecision and instability, for sure. He tries to subtract the facial features belonging to his mother (let's see, the pointy chin will need to be rounded) to get the father. To sketch the face of a stranger, the young man who'd slept with his mother, then (he believed) disappeared. The young man who saw the girl's belly growing and took off, who must have had the same worried expression in the eyes as the son, the same equivocation, the same fierce aimlessness, the same fear, constant and irrational, that he emanates, he the abandoned son, at once absolutely alone in the world and bound by the possessive love of a mother. The night he left home, he thought he'd cut all ties, sliced through them with the suddenness of his unannounced departure, but realized, first in the forest, and later in the shelter of the lighthouse, that these are ties that bind, severed or otherwise.

It's all a jumble in his heart, worse than before, loneliness and dependence, and he has no way out of either. Curled up there inside the dank walls of the tower, what are his hopes, if any, lying there like a hunted animal, his mother trying to track him down, his father, too (has he figured out that part yet?), while he spends his days, isolated and totally on his own, lost among the rocks, in the rustle and rumble of the waves.

And the Meandering Rivers

THE SPECTACLE OF the ocean, it's in my face all day, too, its tire-less convulsions outside my window, shifting and unstable, as if unable to settle into a comfortable position. Forever uneasy, struggling, failing yet again, a restless old animal that won't give up. A kind of old dog turning and turning in a doggy bed that it's outgrown.

There's nothing left for me to do but look, and that's what I'm doing, seated in my armchair, wrapped in a blanket. Not one of those Scottish plaids that immediately spring to mind as soon as you read the word *blanket* (you know how much you want to imagine a woolen weave featuring deep blue, yellow, and red rectilinear patterns whose warm tones add to the coziness of the wool), but instead, a pale monochrome between beige and gray made out of some synthetic fabric in an unidentifiable undulating pattern, in slight relief, so that when you glide your hand over the surface, your palm can feel the sinuous outlines like cresting waves, as if this blanket were meant to represent the ocean on a milky, overcast day, my hand reading in braille its hourly evolution.

Occasionally, under my window, someone will walk past, often with a dog, sometimes two, and hey, that guy, I recognize him, since I see him every day with his three setters, each one yanking on its leash in a different direction, and him in the middle struggling to keep them in step, though his impassive facial expression suggests his mind is on something else entirely, which his walk with the dogs affords him the time to explore, as he mechanically negotiates the dogs' opposing desires—a representation of the dog-walker's interior life in all its contradictions, out there in the salty air, so that we might call each of the dogs and their opposing trajectories by Id, Superego, and Ego, three distinctly individual dogs that he finally reins in, brings together into one, and walks home (and there you go, good boys, into the yard).

Anticipating the rain, maybe, which starts falling just as they leave my field of vision, a sprinkle at first, then a full-blown downpour.

Throughout the expedition, water was all that mattered out there, rainwater and river water that kept the Lewis and Clark team in a stranglehold.

Turns out that rain was an issue from the very start, as it was pouring steadily on the very day of their departure, causing a delay while they waited for the curtain to rise on the scene where they were about to set foot.

They have frightening memories of early days on the Big Muddy, whose banks were collapsing under the force of the driving rains. Entire uprooted trees were carried downstream, some of which flowed just beneath the surface, like submarines, slamming into the hull of your canoe when you never even saw it coming, while others, obeying some law of physics affecting the movement of silt, the speed of the current and the mass of the wood, rose up vertically out of the riverbed like fantastic sea creatures, slick and dark against the backlit pearls of splashing water out of which they emerged; these were the ones liable to overturn their light watercraft when they would well up from underwater hiding place.

Our explorers would then have to stop, necessarily, with the storm tearing down trees all around them. Sitting on the muddy ground, hugging their knees, crouching, starving (impossible to hunt in such weather), they waited out the storm, to the sound of falling tree trunks.

Torrential rain, no escaping it, no corner of the landscape went unscathed, nor were their meager belongings likely to outlast it. They watch as the rain washes away everything in sight, trees tossed into the river that swallowed up and regurgitated, ingested and vomited. What a downpour, they could hardly believe what they were seeing, what a downpour, poor devils; and rain flows not only into the river, into and under their clothing, but into their heads, too. This massive rain, flooding lands and minds, drenching the body and instilling the idea of rain, a singular, masterful idea. Wetness is all that's left in the world, water, water everywhere, seeping into their every thought.

It seems like long ago, that moment of departure, now that they are so close to their goal; but still, rain and more rain, and again, further delays.

They listen to the sound of rain on the wrinkled skin of the river that undulates like a living thing, restless and twisting beneath volleys of water.

Equally hostile is the wind, they don't know how to deal with this nature unleashed.

Oh, and thunder, while we're on the subject.

Whole nights of lightning flashes.

It's getting to be too much. They just want it all to stop. A little rain, a few bumps in the road, that was to be expected, but it's assuming unreasonable proportions.

Nature itself looks different to them now.

Their belongings are covered in mold, fabrics are rotting away, and things are starting to stink.

Rain like hatching veils the view. Massing clouds filter the light. All is dark, obscure, scratched out.

The flora that they'd joyfully set out to identify, gentian and bell-flowers, yeah, right. The truth is sleet, storms, downpours, tree trunks carried by the rapids, crashing into your canoes, which you moor as best you can.

Beached on the pebbly banks of the river, our men still continue to exalt in the notion of finally reaching the ocean, or so claims Clark, who can see nothing beyond his own desire and ambition.

Eventually, though still on the river, there are signs of tidal movement.

That must mean they're getting close.

They get ready.

They look for dry shelter, recesses in the rock where they can crouch and wait, shivering, chilled to the bone, soaking wet, arms around their torsos to keep warm, each hand on the opposite shoulder, as if to console themselves. Jaw muscles contract to keep teeth from chattering. Their clothes are soaking wet, they keep hugging themselves, these little trembling bodies that they've become. Noses run incessantly, too much to sniff back. All is wetness. The only thing missing is tears.

And even they come, sometimes, they would have to, but Lewis and Clark don't see them. They pretend to believe that the final goal of reaching the ocean burns in the heart of every one of these men offered up to the rain, sniffling and coughing into the ill wind.

Let's think positive for a moment. Of course, there was rain, bruises and sprains, hunger and fatigue, but there were also wild berries and deer, sparkling waterfalls in dazzling sunshine, gray-tinted ovals of scattered clouds casting their fleeting shadows over green prairieland, all pretty as a picture, if you manage to forget blistered feet, carbuncles, and your back muscles that register every stroke of the paddle. And the bites.

Because I haven't mentioned those yet, but it goes without saying that, in all that wetness, the Lewis and Clark men had to put up with lots of mosquitoes. And you know what I'm talking about here, those bloody dipterous beasts that aren't content to leave you with itchy, red bites, but seem to delight in hovering over their victims, right before the strike, buzzing around your ears as if to drill into your head what danger lies ahead—oh, how they love it, those evil little pests, the fear they inspire, when your imaginings are triggered.

The expedition was fitted out with plenty of mosquito netting, which they slept under like caterpillars in a cocoon. But the weave wore out, grew moldy with the rains, and tore; the insects rushed into the breaches in the dilapidated fabric and reigned supreme, drunk on the feeding frenzy afforded by these new arrivals from the East, gorging themselves to the edge of nausea (poor babies, with their tummy aches and indigestion).

Sorry, but I can't help it, and there were also fleas that slipped in and out unmolested, hopping here and there, as they do, black, minuscule, and in Olympian form, so well-nourished on all this available flesh, sweaty and salty, covered in a fine layer of filth from so much travel, a feast for the fleas, which took advantage of the bounty, without too much soul searching.

Clark even wrote openly about all the fleas that kept them awake at night.

Sometimes it itched so badly that the men tore their clothes off, shook them furiously, and dove buck naked into the river.

There were also times when they'd climb through the brush, up to a promontory, where they would open their arms wide and offer up their bodies to the rain, screaming; it was a kind of sacrifice, I suppose, a surrender, like a rite of passage, a bizarre cult. They'd climb back down then, and curl up somewhere more sheltered, where their clothing wasn't going to get much drier, in any case, having given up on the very notion of dryness, since the air itself was waterlogged and proved useless.

And there was a further problem when they camped at water's edge, near the mouth of a river. The water would sometimes rise higher than they'd figured it would, and they'd get swamped in the middle of the night. They'd have to get up and drag their soggy bedding further back. And sometimes that wouldn't be enough, and they'd have to do it a second time in one night. They'd grumble, rudely awakened from their dreams by the obstinate wetness of the rising tide that nipped at your ankles beneath the wool, and you'd move a little higher, hoping it'd be enough this time. Wrapped in your shoddy blanket, you'd shiver in the starless night, listening to the water flow slowly over the rocky riverbed.

As soon as there was a ray of sunshine, they tried to dry out their clothes. Fabric scattered over the landscape, occluding it in part, waving in the breeze.

Lovely, these dancing shirts and trousers against the clearing sky; they lie back on a little mound and watch, chewing on some tobacco, taking stock of their recent life history. Summing up the expedition to date, there were thickets, rivers, winds, riverbanks and currents, but also prairies, cactus trees, sorrel and sunflowers and wild cucumber; and again, ash trees and elk, reeds and otters, ryegrass and goslings; there were grouse, they say to themselves, and unripe corn, bison and beaver, copses and catfish, snakes and plovers and fog; a mixed assortment, lowlands and mosquitoes, flintstone and whitlow, low-grade dysentery, green valleys. To which we add horses and dogs, cabins and tents, canoes and foxes, mud and magpies, gauzy skies; frost and dawn's early light, waterfowl, grizzly bears and poplars; you'll also hear them say things like upstream and downstream, overcast weather, guns, chilly nights and great horned owls, sometimes. And don't forget dugouts, quivers, bartering, flag canvas to mend, ice and pebbles, dunes and driftwood. And above all, waiting; and dried meat, rotten meat, very occasionally fish, storms and boulders, and I think that just about does it; and the meandering rivers; and, hopefully, someday, the ocean.

The Benefits of Celluloid

THEY MUST STILL be at it, McCain's men, up there at the homestead, let's not forget them as they keep batting the ball back and forth to tamp down their pent-up resentment against their boss or their memories of a brutal upbringing, as they leap and swat, eyes glued to the white bubble, so fragile and weightless, an image of their lives, shunted around, one hit after another, punched and battered, but always bouncing back, ready to get slammed again by the brutally indifferent paddle that sends it back, like a refusal, a rejection; and on it goes, rebuffed and refused until it misses the table surface altogether and spins beyond reach. It ricochets off the cement patio, pathetic and ashamed, and a few bounces later, hits the wall and comes to a stop in a gutter, of course, where some stagnant rainwater has pooled, and there it lies, stained, wet, dirty and alone. Until someone goes to recover it, because the ordeal isn't over yet; the ball is soon back in play—take that, and that—I'm telling you, it's a metaphor for their lives.

What you should know is that ping-pong balls serve another purpose, too.

Most of the time, it's in the evening, after dinner.

One of the gang goes out to the garage and gets a roll of tin foil (the kitchen kind, nothing fancy), while the others collect old ping-pong balls that are dying a slow death in gutters and elsewhere, on and around the patio, forgotten and weathered by the rain. In the dark, their whiteness is almost phosphorescent.

Here's how they go about it.

You tear off a piece of foil (it doesn't always cut cleanly against the serrated blade, I know, so do your best), place a ping-pong ball in the center, like so, then fold in the foil, be careful, around a pencil to get the shape of a chimney. Good. Now, remove the pencil.

They make several like that, using the ping-pong table as their workstation, which is practical.

Then, they go out to the grassy area in the backyard. They each take out a cigarette lighter.

What you need to know is that ping-pong balls are made of celluloid, a composite, which I'll explain, of nitrocellulose and camphor, to which is mixed a dash of solvent (usually ethyl alcohol). In other words, a highly flammable, insanely explosive material which, and this isn't the least of its charms, is likely to produce a large amount of gas.

Using your lighter, you heat the aluminum foil from below, and what comes through the chimney is an abundance of toxic, white smoke.

The men throw their smoke bombs, caught up in the effect they're producing, gazing up at the thick swirls climbing into the damp Oregon skies.

Who knows what it is that puts them in the mood to manufacture smoke bombs, in the evening, looking all conspiratorial, with that low, dumbass laugh of theirs as they lob the bombs and watch dreamily as the white smoke rises heavenward.

It's a pastime like any other, you might say.

But it's also possible that, using a remote firing device, or even without using one, just throwing the projectile barehanded, if that's what it takes, these balls might be a great way to smoke out McCain's victims in a room in their house, or in their car, or any other enclosed place. The procedure is pretty foolproof

and leaves no trail: once combustion is complete, the ball inside
the foil wrapper has totally disappeared.

And maybe this is what our guys get to thinking, as they stare
up at the swirling smoke's ascent into the night sky. As the celluloid melts away in each foil packet, as their eyes follow the
opal emanations that spiral into the darkness, the men feel a
rush of excitement at the looming threat they have launched
above the town.

Maybe they're also thinking about McCain, asleep, his
slumbering body alone in his room. About the day when they'll
aim their missiles at him, all together, and then make themselves
scarce.

The Frog

THAT'S ALL WELL and good, melting ping-pong balls by the light
of the moon and all, but I'm going to have to say what I've been
meaning to say from the start, but keep putting off—even if,
so that you understand exactly what it's all about, so that you
know, to whatever degree I'm able to get it across, all the ins and
outs of the issue, even if you also had to learn a little something
about the folks living in Cannon Beach. Which is why it hasn't
been a waste of time to have you spend a few evenings at Moses's
place, to watch me thinking things through out there on the
wooden steps in front of the bar, sorting out all the stories I had
just heard, to let you in on the details of Colter's upbringing,
his story with Betty, and everything you're beginning to find out
about Shannon, what you've learned about Mary, but also about
Harry Dean, or Perry, and since she has meant something to all
of them, Wendy, even though I've only ever seen her once, the
day I arrived, since I've never been back to the Blueberry after
that, and why should I have. And even about McCain's posse,
them in particular, I'd even say.

So, by way of an ending, and to wrap up the series of the clues
and signs that marked the months spent between the motel and
Moses's bar, there's one more thing I have to tell, a kind of lame
joke told by Colter, a joke aimed at me, that is, a blunder, I
think we can safely call it a blunder, even if you keep your sense
of humor and say it's no big deal, peanuts, which is what I did,
just let bygones be bygones, because that's how I am, probably,
a forgive-and-forget kind of guy.

It was a day when Colter started talking about the house again.

Because his house wasn't only that building open to the four winds, windows broken, that it had perhaps become, its useless pediments set against the ruthless skies; nor was it only the empty shell he'd entered one day, where everything he had ever wanted to build had collapsed in an instant: it was also the memory of the glorious day when he had closed the deal, the day that was supposed to have been day one of his happy new life that held out so much promise, and that Colter clutched close to his heart like an injured sparrow, that's the comparison that springs to mind, a frail, quivering bird, one of its legs broken, that you'd hold in your hand and feel trembling.

That kind of happiness, no matter what happens to it later, Colter repeated, you can never forget it; and he'd start in describing the house, as if it were still there. And that afternoon with the bank loan officer, the beige cloth satchel he'd purchased just for the occasion, a carrying case for all the paperwork, which made him seem more worldly and serious-minded (how many times had he retold it, that scene of triumph with the banker, and then with the notary, always mentioning the satchel as a token of his success, his earnestness, his unlikely credibility), the pouch where he slipped the signed dossier, sitting there in a bank office (imagine a large window with slatted shades to filter the light, an impeccable chiaroscuro, and the two of them bathed in these sumptuous stripes) (you'd swear you were on a movie set), slowly fastening the clasps, he was in no hurry, savoring this moment when he, the kid thrown out of his childhood home by the fake father, felt he was finally getting his revenge. During this minute or so when the banker (and later, the notary) was attending to his every need, Colter could afford to take his time, scrupulously slipping the strap through the buckle, there you go, pulling it nice and tight, good, and then doing the same on the other side, carefully, solemnly, then gripping the satchel by the handle and raising his eyes to meet those of the man in the suit and tie, as if to say, okay, we can go now (since it was Colter who was setting the tempo here); then, the man in the three-piece rose and came around his desk, walked Colter down the hall to the exit, and held the door for him—ah, moments like that one, Colter sighed, leaving the sentence unfinished.

Still, and this is my point, the house, with the grandiose trilogy of its pediments he so lovingly described to anyone who'd listen, the immaculate garage door, and the bulbous bow window jutting harmlessly into the yard that extended uninterrupted out to the street, featured yet another ornament, the ultimate token of Colter's success, nailed to the front door, a shiny brass knocker that I know I've already mentioned, and that particular night, Colter thought it appropriate to add a further detail to his description: the brass knocker was in the form of a frog, all crouched and round-backed, perfectly ergonomic for the hand when you draped your fingers over it and held it in your palm; because that's what you did, Colter raved, you took the little critter into your hand (your eye drawn to the polished metal that caught the evening light that glinted off its surface, prestige writ large, the sign that Colter had arrived), and banged that sucker down on the door, as many times as it took (the harder the better, so that they heard you inside), you didn't hold back, and why should you, asked Colter (was he already looking at me at this point), that's what the little amphibian was there for, to take hits, to make noise, that metal-on-metal knocker noise.

Colter, you'll recall, when he would go home at night, instead of using his key, he preferred to knock, just for the kick of having the door opened by the three that he'd bought the house for (Betty and the two kids, like three diamonds in the pastel jewel box of his little dream house), which meant that, if he were keeping score, declared Colter, he must have hit that son of a gun hundreds of times, maybe thousands. And just as he said that, there was a strange glimmer in his eye, like some evil creature lodged in his pupil, in the pitch dark, that suddenly decided to turn on the lights, declaring I live here, after all, right?

Sure, the poor frog had taken some hard knocks (hah hah), so what was his point, I was wondering, and I couldn't tell if he'd realized it from the start, or if it had slowly dawned on him, after telling the story so many times, a gradual percolation of this word *frog* that had been working its way up, unbeknownst to him, into his pre-conscious mind, before he understood that what really tickled him the most was the endless repetition of the word *frog*, to tell how the poor frog would keep getting the crap beat out of it, pow! right in the face, because that was its job, right? And as I was sitting there, drinking my beer and listening to him ramble on, it never occurred to me that I too was a frog. Then, all of a sudden, it clicked with him, and Colter looked at me, and that glimmer in his eye from a moment ago sharpened to beam. Hey, you're a froggy, ain't you? he said, slapping his thighs, and that's when it came back to me, that we're called *froggies*, for reasons I've never really understood, because, I don't know about you, but for me personally, I've eaten frog legs exactly twice in my whole life, the first time in an Asian restaurant, and the second, at the home of a woman from British Guiana. Statistically, it's never seemed to me like a particular feature of French cuisine, but some Brit must have thought so one day, and the word spread, from pub to pub, reaching into every corner of Great Britain, then over to America, where it eventually made its way over the river and through the woods, all the way to Cannon Beach, and there it was, making its appearance at the stuffy *Ulysses*, as Colter held forth, sounding more incoherent by the minute, free-associating his brass knocker into yours truly, whom he had reduced, like a shrunken head, down to the size of the hopping amphibian, to be held in the palm and pounded on the door. He started pointing at me, saying, *frog*, with that sudsy beer laugh he gets, and he was clearly making the connection between the palmed frog knocker, and me getting slammed against the front door, again and again, an endless ordeal, the little Frenchie hurled into the door, behind which there would one day soon be no one left to open it for him, and I seemed to be the designated victim that would have to pay for all that.

I pictured the shiny little frog hovering above the threshold, then Colter's hand taking hold of it, banging it against the door, I looked into his bloodshot eyes, everyone's eyes that night (and this is only a slight exaggeration) looked to me like a pack of wolves, eyes shining in the deep night forest.

Moses, true to form, was working persistently to remove a stubborn spot from a beer mug; it seemed to be taunting him; though you'd think a spot would be keeping a low profile, given the prospect of a rag coming at you with full force, you can only imagine what that must feel like, cotton weave rubbing and rubbing, the rubber's single objective being to annihilate you. Can we imagine the fear that spot must be feeling, what it means to be struggling with all its might against the forces of obliteration?

The Blinding Light of Iraq

AFTER ALL, IT could just as easily have ended right there.

With that little joke, a malicious one, I have to say, about the frog-shaped brass knocker, and the uneasiness I sometimes felt, a sense of something remaining unresolved, but which might have persisted as only a shading, a nuance, a fleeting, pointless concern, something that might have shadowed those days without any real consequence.

But there was something else that Shannon had been mumbling over in his corner, and I'm not setting up a cause and effect here, no, I'm just saying that it didn't help.

What Shannon was mumbling, apart from the hypothetical story of his runaway son's dubious existence among the pines, apart from the yet-to-be-elucidated fight scene in the forest that Shannon couldn't help alluding to every so often, was the story of the brother.

Shannon's brother was named Rick (Rick, Shannon said to me one day, jabbing his finger at me, like I had something to do with it). The "r" unfurled like a drum roll, while the "ick" shot out sharp, strangled in mid-syllable, it sounded hostile and warlike in Shannon's mouth. Especially since, and I haven't had a chance to mention this, but when you listen closely, behind his alcohol-saturated mishmash of syllables, you noticed a slight speech defect that he probably also had when he was sober—though I've never had an opportunity to verify that—something bad enough to keep him from speaking out, and not only at the bar, but even as a teenager, it's possible, and even when he would phone the mother of his first son, when he'd shut himself into the glass phone booth and watch the dun-colored world through the dirty panes, through greasy halos that distorted the passersby, feeling so overwhelmed by this new responsibility, so unprepared, so under attack by her blustery, inconsistent rejection, even then, with this woman shouting on the other end (he looked, puzzled, at the loose metallic cord leading from the receiver, through which passed all those needlessly aggressive words, pushing through the twisted cable like cars on a roller coaster, fast and bumpy), even then he'd feel the added shame of someone having to hear the gravelly sound of his own voice that even he himself couldn't stand, fast rapids on a pebbly stream, tongue hitting palate in the wrong place; what caused the slight torque of the words coming out of Shannon's mouth, turning everything he said into a shipwreck? And there he'd be in the phone booth, his weight on one leg, other knee slightly bent, looking like a Saint Sebastian, offering his bared body to the slings and arrows that the woman was shooting into his flesh with the same ferociousness as that of the invisible archer, outside the frame, zing! zing! zing! with no thought as to the slaughter they're causing (oozing wounds, you know, those poppy-red trails of blood on the martyr's milky skin), thinking it best to simply hang up. It took Mary's fringed skirt for Shannon to speak his mind, and then, the sarcasm would gush forth before he could even remember how distorted the words coming from his mouth would be, and since he has a loud voice, you might conclude that anger alone accounted for his twisty, incomplete delivery.

Getting back to Rick, to the gravelly roll his name produced in Shannon's mouth, Rick who, as a teenager, would often leave home for a few days, before returning hungry and haggard, falling back into his household habits until the next breakaway; Rick who, when he was old enough, aware of the economic misery all around him, and wanting to make a cleaner, more definitive break with the family, enlisted in the army, where they promised he'd be set for life.

He did this without telling anyone, without giving his parents the chance to help him weigh the pros and cons, his mother perhaps attempting to hold him back, his father, motivated by some vague sense of fatherly pride, encouraging the son (who would have been caught in the middle, better not to tell them at all). He came back one afternoon, packed his bags and told them he was joining the army. No hugs or tears, nothing about furloughs, how he'd be spending his leave, whether he'd ever come home to see them.

Naturally, the parents wondered if he'd done it for the salary, or was it because of them; they thought back to all the times he'd run away, and how, whenever he came back, they'd act as if he'd never left, no questions asked, no reproach. Was he annoyed that they were so easy on him, did he take it as a sign of disinterest, of indifference? Rick was the only one who ever raised his voice, but he could never get a rise out of them, they just let him do as he pleased—not important, he'll grow out of it (he'll grow out of it, that was the silent mantra they'd repeat to themselves, and he must have figured it out just by looking at their placid faces, mirror of the fatalistic, hands-off way that they ignored whatever he said. And it must have been excruciating for him). They put up with his abuse, out of love probably, but what about him? Did he feel the family around him like a loose net full of holes that couldn't prevent him from falling if he happened to fall? Is that what he was searching for, an authority figure, as they say, the great brainwashing exercise of blind obedience, of surrendering all decision-making? Did he yearn to sink into submission, or even better than sinking, to disappear, to dissolve, become passive and interchangeable, as long as there was someone stronger than you that you could depend on, because authority's harsh words, which might well break him, could also keep him in check and hold him together, in the end?

There he'd be in the family living room with his suppressed rage, not knowing where to turn (to the father, lying mute on the sofa? to his mother, with her kindly absent gaze? Shannon, who must have been how old at the time, an unreliable confidant, perhaps?), Rick, standing there on the carpet, stiff and trembling, deliriously lonely and not knowing why, laid low before their amorphous bodies that seemed poised in expectation of something that would never come (or worse, they had given up hoping for anything at all, a vision he simply could not bear), Rick left home to immerse himself in the tough, sweat-soaked milieu one imagines the army to be, bodies engaged in direct action (but in inaction, too, lots of inaction, those long waiting patterns), a brutal brotherhood, flawed and ambiguous, in tedium as in fear, in the midst of men noisily asserting their bodies.

Maybe he was thinking of it as a chance to travel, since the army does offer, if nothing else, a change of scene.

Searing skies, strong sunshine, a complete switch from soggy Oregon. That's what they show in their promotional fliers, men in combat fatigues against exotic backgrounds, places they could never dream of going if it weren't for the army sending them there.

And travel he did.

He walked across the military airport tarmac and up the steps into the plane, turning around to gaze one last time at the gray, waterlogged sky that he was about to trade in for another, relentless and fierce, that would bounce off whitewashed walls and sand, causing him to squint to shield his eyes from the searing light.

The intense heat, the uncompromisingly blue skies, uninterruptedly blue, impermeable, stretched across the desert's dry skin.

Palm trees forming asterisks against the sky, and something

he wasn't expecting: green. For there were floodplains and marshlands (yes, there were those), groves of fruit trees where birds flew and nested as they had always done (or had things changed for them?), though now, with the noise and dust from the gunfire that interrupted their daily flight patterns, the birds must have noticed that it was more complicated out there than usual, and that when they pierced the fruits with their beaks, was there not a new smell, or what exactly, a burnt smell, that was it, they would swallow the bit of smoky-flavored fruit, the bitter taste of war, down into their little stomachs, what else were they supposed to do.

He must have been doing some hard thinking, Rick, behind those sunglasses, as he watched the place get blown to bits (sunglasses that he'd purchased right before departure, checking them out in the little mirror attached to the carousel display to see how they looked on him, with their metal frames and extra-dark lenses that turned the world a smoky brown, the necessary fiction-making filter between the outside world and himself, whenever the plunge into reality was at its most brutal, whenever his body was most exposed). He'd wanted to travel, and this is what he got, blowing things up as per the orders of his lieutenant-in-command, whose directives could not have been clearer.

Waking up every morning under a tent, long days with nothing to do, and when an attack finally does come, a state of excitement, almost joy, that what you're doing is legitimate and justified, since this is what you trained for, what you've been waiting all this time for, that action and aggressiveness that society has asked you to repress is now being demanded of you, and sometimes, as you dash through bursts of machine-gun fire, you even get the feeling you're in a war movie, that confused state of unreality that takes over (what you are thinking in order to fire, or not thinking, what you absolutely shouldn't be thinking, as you pull the trigger and focus only on how best to absorb the recoil); and Rick, suddenly under the lights, also under fire, but it must have felt like he was under the lights, the kliegs, since, in order to do what they're being told to do, they have to convince themselves that this is only a movie, and they're just Hollywood extras being followed around by a camera in a fake war zone, and each one of them thinks he's the hero of the shot, and off they go into battle, the chief cameraman shouldering his Steadicam, following right behind, and you're being shot at while he's shooting you shooting, and cut, it looks like a wrap, so how did I do?

The fierce beauty of the landscape in perpetual summer can make you crazy. That, and the authorized violence, basically the military-issue license to kill, to march across this land with an M4 strapped across your chest, a reliable, handy assault weapon (rotary breech, telescoping buttstock, full automatic firing, some serious gear, in other words) (one helpful piece of advice: make sure you mount the telescopic sight into the designated groove) worn across the body, bobbing on your bulletproof vest that you wear over your cotton camouflage fatigues, in that ever-familiar sycamore bark pattern (*my cammies*, say the guys, who never wear anything else) (and on your belt, you've got your Beretta M9), and all that hardware, full battle rattle, completely outfitted for combat, including your thick-soled rangers that kick up the sand as if it were nothing at all.

And when the sun goes down and you're just so sick of it all, you drink, sing, and joke around, while the *khamsin* shakes your tent flaps, and the starry sky above acts like nothing has happened.

Rick, sure, I can picture him, he's strange to me the way two brothers can be to one another. A testy, helpless guy, like all soldiers that are victims of far more than enemy shelling. Rick was already a mess, in any case, and had to struggle against the idea that he was falling apart, crumbling into the sand and smoke (something inside was dead, and had no chance of rebirth) (almost no chance, he held out the slimmest hope). What was going through Rick's head, underneath that helmet, what was gnawing at his innards, something that the fear of death alone could temporarily dispel (it didn't relieve him, but just took up all the room—already a kind of relief—otherwise occupied by unthinkable thoughts), and if only you knew, Shannon, how vividly I was imagining your brother, how distinctly I could feel his panic and jubilation, the psychic devastation there must have been.

Pulling the trigger, Rick let loose whatever it was he'd been holding back, and he knew that was how it had to be, that they had to take it for the others, the inhabitants of Iraq (or no, you weren't supposed to say the inhabitants, or the civilians, whom we were supposed to be there to protect, you were supposed to say Iraqi combatants) (but we knew, we could see it before our eyes, that we were also killing women and children), they'd take it for our inadequate parents, for the tone-deaf, spineless father, for the bedraggled mother, who hadn't been able to protect him, for the morose streets of the little town where he grew up, where the neighbors bummed around, unemployed, they'd be taking it for all that.

But Rick didn't get the chance to take his vengeance all the way. He was cut down in action, out there in Iraq, where the American soldiers couldn't get their graft to take, rejection after rejection, nothing would stick, you might say, and Shannon's brother was rejected along with everyone else, his body pierced by a bullet in the desert of Iraq, beneath a red-hot sky that exacerbates all physical sensation.

Over there, where the French had opted not to go (the French, with their built-in skepticism, their superiority complex, while

Rick believed the WMD farce, because everyone over here did, in America, they all bought it), Rick, the brother, found warmth, and searing sun, and a taste for torture, but died in the process.

That night, Shannon talked about his brother, and it struck me again, like a bolt of lightning, and as hard as it had that first night I encountered the three of them at the *Ulysses*, that they might be looking for a fight, because Shannon might want me to pay for that death, for all the French soldiers who hadn't been there to take the bullet instead of his brother, who came home in a big, flag-draped casket, a red, white and blue tablecloth, and for everything that ensued, the mother's tears, the devastated father, who stopped speaking altogether. In that oceanic night, the blackest of skies, they could have taken it all out on me, avenged the brother's death, a pointless, boneheaded, hidebound vengeance, as if each blow that failed to resuscitate something of the brother, which they all knew was impossible, would at least ratify his death, provide justification for his and all the other GI deaths, get that through your thick skull, fucking Frenchie, soon to be beaten to a pulp beneath the American skies.

McCain Returns

I DID NOTHING out of the ordinary that day. I must have taken a walk on the beach, probably not a long one, because of the violence of the elements along that coast, where anything resembling a peaceful stroll is impossible, ruining an otherwise carefree jaunt in a light sea breeze, the waves tickling the sand, because tickling is exactly what they never do, they beat the holy hell out of the sand, they brutalize it; and the same goes for the wind that whips you like a cat-o'-nine-tails coming at you from all directions, unbridled and invisible, tangling you up in its lashes.

So why keep doing it, as I did again that morning, exposing my body to this constant hostility, to the monstrous aggressiveness of the beach, with the ocean that keeps rising up, its gray-green fabric snapping in the wind, like some iconic representation of menace? I must have then walked down the main street, sheltered from the wind at that point, to buy myself a chicken burger to go, yes, that's it, go back to my room to eat it, maybe take a nap, who knows how the hours pass here, sleeping the time away in this land's-end type of place where, when you open your eyes again onto the picture window and beyond, all you see is the mute spectacle of the waves under a boundless sky, with only the idea of Japan on the far side.

It was starting to get dark by the time I was walking over to the *Ulysses*. The sky was turning anthracite, and felt narrow-minded somehow: not even the slightest fantasy (no burst of orange for that fireworks effect, no streak of lightning, nothing), only the pale gray of daylight, compact and even, that was slowly darkening.

Lamps were starting to blink on indoors, windows lighting up their little squares in increasing numbers as the day waned. I don't know what was on my mind at the time. At each orthogonal cross street, I felt a blast of beach—wind and all that ocean racket—hit me from the side, before walking back into the protective canyon of walls on either side, temporary protection, at best.

I was inhabited by the same feelings as always, on all those nights when I'd walk by those same facades separating me from the ocean's rumble that the side streets channeled. That same old mix of soothing sameness of place and the persistent strangeness of its décor (those clapboard storefronts that I'd brush by, the pressure of the tides, trees turned inside out by the prevailing winds, the guardian rock), a growing, imperfect familiarity, bound to remain unfamiliar because of that necessary distance (shortened though it was by each day I spent there) between these people in their goose-down jackets who talk among themselves in their language, and me (their language, which channeled other histories, other sagas), because of what accompanied me at all times in the streets of Cannon Beach, the muffled realization, both exhilarating and hurtful, that I wasn't from around here. But that realization was no greater or lesser than any other time, nor was the wind any stronger or weaker, nor was the darkening sky any bigger or smaller, and night fell as always.

And there was that same dampness as I entered the dimly lit premises where everything conspired (the yeasty smell of beer, the salty air that burst in every time the door opened, our mingling breaths) to create that thick, wet, stuffy texture we were all steeping in.

Shannon was already there, recently joined by Colter and

Harry Dean, who had come straight from the Blueberry with their usual slate of fresh news (Wendy, and all that)—nothing we didn't already know, one buttock perched on the barstool, something in their body language saying they'd just gotten out of a vehicle, something remembered in muscle and mind of the half-hour or so spent in the truck driving through the woods down to the coast, pine trees parading by, their backs settled into the seat, the single centerline there to make you feel like you're getting somewhere, and the most recent satisfaction, after slamming the truck door closed, to have made it to your destination. Some flash in their eyes spoke momentarily of the euphoria they always felt during the first minutes of any evening at the *Ulysses* with their buddies, prior to the inevitable relapse.

And Moses putting down his towel to serve me up a beer, and the guys saying hello: all pretty routine, I might have thought.

Because that night at the *Ulysses*, and here's what's important, you could say that everything started out normally. No sign, not a hint, it's undisputable, absolutely nothing unusual in the air: Shannon wore his usual frown (another fight with Mary? Nothing came up in conversation), nothing new about that, and nothing anyone could do about it. Moses drying his same mugs, twisting the towel round and round in each. Then, for a change of pace, Tim, who we didn't see that often at the bar, must have thought to himself, after finishing his bowl of micro-waved instant soup, that he didn't much feel like spending the evening in front of the TV, so I'll just slip on my jacket and go on down, not even a stop at the shop, how about going over to the *Ulysses* and knocking back a couple (this is Tim talking to himself), which is just what he did, he joined the group, in his own discreet way, quiet and just a little anxious.

I'm thinking I haven't said enough about Tim so far, but this really isn't the time to, that night when everything was going to change all at once, the night I've been wanting to talk about all along, the one I have to tell you about, but have been putting it off for a while now, since you had to know something about all the people involved.

Tim, if he had been more of a regular at Moses's place, you'd have found out more about him, so it's partially his fault, but since we're on the subject, I'll tell you a couple quick things about Daisy, so that you'll get why Tim is so quiet, because there's a story behind that silence. Tim had lived for years with Daisy, a plump, gabby woman who was always talking in his place. Tim, himself an average talkative type when they'd first met, spoke less and less as the weeks and months went by. Think of it as a long decrescendo in his use of the spoken word, until the time came when he was barely saying ten sentences in a whole day, and even then, only the most utilitarian, and only if he absolutely had to. At the same time, the woman's gabbiness rate increased steadily, until she got so bored with this person who sat there and said nothing that she left him.

Tim didn't go back to talking, though. But he did grow more anxious, an anxiety with no obvious basis, a little like animals always on the lookout for a rustling of leaves, even though they live in a place where the sound of wind rustling leaves is a constant background noise.

The guys drank beer after beer, no different from any other night, saying the same things they always said, in the same dank barroom air, the same smell of sweat and hops.

And outside, now and since time immemorial, the sound of the breakers, the same raw presence of churning water indicating that turmoil is the baseline state of things here. That night, the waves took their usual running start and then crashed down on the beach, but when had it ever been any different?

I was chasing one beer with another, not expecting anything unusual to happen, when McCain burst through the door of the *Ulysses*.

McCain, unchanged, with that prying look of his, those wrinkles across his face that drew a pictogram of the waves outside, a tattoo etched into his mulish forehead.

This time, he'd brought a sidekick, a big, heavyset, round-faced guy with two little piercing eyes that seemed to be straining to concentrate on their surroundings and send messages about what they saw back to his brain, which labored to interpret them, but all that took time, it looked a little too complicated for the slow-witted oaf to process.

Had to be one of the henchmen, working tonight as bodyguard, and who may have been present at other times, but had stayed outside, behind the door, ready to intervene, beaming those same two eyes (the only ones he had) into the Cannon Beach night, scanning for potential danger, so devoted was he.

That night, McCain had taken a different tack from that first time: no more tedious lectures (praising the green meadows of Ireland, as you'll recall) behind which you sensed a hidden agenda that you weren't sure how to decode; no, this time, it was stony silence. Not like Shannon's silence (inward-looking, bound up in personal issues), or not even like Tim's (anxious silence, unsure that what he had to say would matter), but a silence meant to unnerve, silence with intent, a targeted silence, creating the kind of suspense where a single word becomes an event.

Because that's what McCain was trying to do, become an event.

With two fingers up, he ordered for them both (the other guy remaining scrupulously unexpressive, as if it took superhuman focus just to keep his face evenly vacant, a blank slate no one could read anything into).

Colter, Shannon, Harry Dean, Tim, who had all stopped what they were doing (turned toward him now, docile and expectant), were now resuming their interrupted conversations, those well-rehearsed randomly linked phrases on the same old themes, whose many variations I had heard innumerable times (you know them by now, abandonment, break-ups, desperate hope sunk into a piece of real estate, the wild urge to get the hell out of there that ferments in all of us).

The kid in the photo continued to watch Moses's every move, with that same stoically fearful look in the eyes. McCain's presence was making me uneasy, so I focused on those eyes, and what struck me that night was the notion that there was some kind of tacit contract between Moses and the kid. Like a promise to be faithful, or maybe something even stronger, like a real contract, the kind you make with a hitman. Maybe it involved a matter of vengeance that Moses had to play out when the time was right.

The child had to be avenged, that was it, and Moses kept the photo in view as a reminder of the miniature person he once was; always there behind him, to make sure he didn't forget his commitment or go back on his word. To make sure the boy and the man were the same person, one a little older than the other, differently proportioned, but still the same; this is what the child wanted with all his heart.

But truth is (it jumped right out at you), difference was everywhere. The face had thickened, grown hair, and Moses's bulk contrasted sharply with the child's frail body. And that's what I finally understood that night. This critical transformation, an irreversible flaw that erased all traces of the childhood self, this was exactly what the child had feared, this is what caused the trembling, pleading smile. He was afraid of disappearing into adulthood, a change soon to come that would annihilate him, return him to an ancient, dead form.

That's what struck me that night as I stared at the photo. I was overwhelmed by an acute sadness that bore into my chest, as if I were mourning something, which I was, in fact, since that smiling, confused child with the scrawny little torso is a child no one will ever see again: that child, no matter what we do, that child is gone.

Afterward, what triggered the events that followed, I'm still trying to figure out, even now. The comment that lit McCain's fuse—or was it a move someone made—setting the rest in motion, unstoppable. Or maybe McCain had orchestrated the whole thing, because that's the question for which there is no clear answer, whether it was a chain of random events, or whether McCain had come down that night to make it happen.

After a certain number of beers, everybody usually feels like they understand one another. But it's like those prescription drugs that sometimes have the opposite effect from the one intended: deep in the heart of this improvised brotherhood, feeding on fermented barley and hops, the slithering snake of paranoia is stirred.

That's what seemed to be happening in McCain's head. The little snake had awoken, shaken off its sleep, and uncoiled before us, raising its head to have a look around. It was through these snake eyes that McCain was assessing the situation.

Between him and me, there were about two body widths, and he kept a close eye on this gap, making it increasingly obvious that he was checking. It occurred to me that he was thinking about everything that kept us apart, the width of an entire continent plus the Atlantic, I who had come all this way to end up on an empty beach whose sole pride was its gigantic boulder. He made the mental journey in the opposite direction, and it seemed so remote to him that he wondered whether I wasn't made out of a different stuff from him.

Outside, the ocean must have been in full pounding mode, and with one thing leading to another, was it the froth on the beer and the foam of the waves that made McCain snap?

I don't know, maybe I was just suddenly overwhelmed by fatigue and the lateness of the hour, the amount of beer I'd drunk, or was it just that I felt defeated all of a sudden, but something had paralyzed my will, like in those bad dreams when you sense danger coming, and when it finally does, instead of fleeing, you head right into it, classic nightmare logic.

McCain had caught my pupils in the laser beam of his gaze, and it was at that point I knew there would be no escape.

His gray-blue eyes then did a sweep of everyone assembled in the bar, and it was like that announcement you make at weddings, that officially worded imperative, spoken aloud for all to hear, it was as if McCain had demanded that if anyone had anything to say, now was the time to say it, or forever hold their peace.

Nobody said a word, so McCain gave a signal to his sidekick.

So the bodyguard took me outside, and everyone else followed, including, of course, McCain, from whose house up the mountain you could have watched the whole scene, if it had taken place in the daytime, but also Shannon, and Harry Dean, and Colter (Moses stayed inside), and Tim too, who stood back a bit, something in his face both disapproving and cowardly, an unfinished expression, a pathetic, fence-sitting face that said not to look his way for help.

The others surrounded us, McCain's bruiser and me in the center, like some folk dance where they form a circle, then send two people into the middle to dance, and they watch and clap and encourage, except that what the two of us were about to do was anything but dancing.

I had just enough time to wonder exactly what it was we were expected to do out there, and what it all meant, since the guy didn't seem to be in any hurry, but just looked me up and down, less out of strategic interest than a desire to lend a certain solemnity to the proceedings. And in that short interval, I tried but frankly could not understand how things had come to this.

None of the guys intervened, though I couldn't say they were siding with the other guy either (they just stood there in silence), or even that there was anything mean in their look: their eyes dull and lifeless, their faces submissive and resigned to the inevitable, a bunch of dead-ender fatalists.

They looked on, as if they had known all along that this day would come.

If it hadn't been that night with that particular McCain stooge, it would have been some other night, with a different guy, just as ready and willing to do his boss's bidding.

What McCain's flunky was preparing to do as they watched is what all of them could have done on that first night I showed up at the *Ulysses*, when things might have taken a nasty turn, if I really think back; and even later, I never did gain any ground, all those nights, hour after hour, when I thought I'd finally earned my place, and later still, if I really thought back on it, with Shannon and his brother in Iraq, and the French, who refused to lend a hand, the French, who let his brother die, and I was lumped together with them, in Shannon's mind, me with the French. And even Colter, and his frog story, Colter, who thought it was so hysterically funny to slam a frog against the door, even Colter, who'd occasionally sit out on the stoop in front of the bar after closing, shoulder to shoulder, and remember that whole issue about the American flag planted on the moon that I said I couldn't see, all of this flashed through my mind, us sitting there on the steps looking at the lumpy old moon where Colter was sure you could make out the flag that Armstrong had pounded into the lunar soil for the honor of all Americans.

As I exited the bar, pushed forward by McCain's hitman, didn't I have time to see the knocker in Colter's gaze, the little brass frog that shone with a metallic gleam?

As for Harry Dean, that enigmatic slim-Jim of a dude, not a peep from him either, and everything he knew about volcanoes, or about the Lewis and Clark expedition, thanks to Perry, none of that did him any good that night: he just stood there like the others, a passive bystander, as if he were somewhere else.

You could hear the waves close by, relentless, hostile, but assiduous. The sound of the ocean carried on the sudden gust of wind had the effect of a command.

The guy came at me swinging.

At first, it was just slaps, all of which he landed (since I didn't know how to protect myself), and an occasional hook, to surprise me, I suppose, but nothing surprised me (I didn't know the first thing about boxing), except this whole situation itself, this moment of insanity beneath the Cannon Beach sky, getting beat up by this stranger, encircled by the guys I'd spent almost all my evenings with here.

But there was something disingenuous about my surprise, since, deep down, I knew that things were going to end like this.

You have to believe that these guys jones for a good fight every once in a while, when you live there on the oceanfront, with the waves coming at you with that grinding roar, that relentless pounding sound, while life here seems leaden, stuck in time, empty, nothing to do. McCain's man was having himself a field day, taking his time, savoring the moment.

The pain is hard to describe, how piercing it is, oddly sharp and dull at the same time. But it wasn't only the physical pain: while this guy was beating the shit out of me, taking short pauses so that it wouldn't be over too soon, it was their presence, their silent assent, how they just allowed it to happen.

That was more painful than the bruising I was getting, the chilling picture of their bodies standing there, unmoved, in the oceanic night.

Me in the middle, getting slowly demolished, and them out there in their circle, motionless, taking it all in, no rage but no pity either, passively accepting the rules that McCain had laid down. Pow! And every punch was like the expression of the now

deeply rooted fact that I had no business in this place, a fact that
they had never really dislodged from their brains.

You could still hear the ocean crashing down on the beach,
and it was as if that acidic ocean water was what coursed through
their veins. McCain's gorilla just kept at it, assiduous, precise,
and brutal, by the light of the moon that cast a silvery edging
onto the massive darkness of his body that seemed to be giving
off a halo of electricity.

With the pain came numbness. I sensed myself moving away
from the scene; I felt absent, is how I felt. About to pass out, as
the reality of it all began to fade (the dark silhouette of the guy
outlined in a bluish-silver halo), I felt something withdrawing
from my body, and that something was me, I was slowly slipping
outside myself, slowly extinguishing the me inside me, leaving
behind, in front of that clapboard building, on the muddy
blacktop, at the feet of those I'd spent so many hours with in the
dank atmosphere of Moses's bar, listening to each of them tell
the dismal story of his fucked-up life, nothing but the bloody
pulp of my former self. The heart was still beating, but for the
moment, there was nobody home.

On the Beach

I WOKE UP on the beach.

I don't know which one of them dragged me out there, a certain distance from the bar, probably first making sure I was still breathing (if they even bothered to wonder).

The sea air whipped at my face and carcass, and eventually brought me to.

It took me a little while to remember.

The sun was coming up, clouds were racing by overhead, looking almost harried, against the pale blue sky.

I sat up on the sand as best as I could manage. My whole body ached.

The ocean had retreated, regrouping. It was low tide, which of course was not going to last, but for the time being, it was in no hurry to come roaring back; in fact, it seemed to be dragging its feet a little, way out there, in the dawn's early light.

And then it all came back.

I remembered the little snake in McCain's eye.

It was undoubtedly the kind of serpent that had been there all along, coiled up and waiting to spring. Buried there in McCain's body, where it had taken up residence so long ago that no one could have put a date on it. And he had no intention of dislodging it, no sir. He pampered it, fed it, and sometimes let it have its say. Under those conditions, it would have been impolite for the snake to desert its host.

In the evening, it found new vigor at the watering hole, where it became distinctly visible in the eye, ready to pounce and bite.

I'd located that snake in McCain from the very start. It was up to no good, undulating with pleasure, and in that dance was something hideously precise.

So, why did I just stand there like an idiot, when I could see what was lurking behind those eyes, why was I frozen in place?

Couldn't I have just gone right up to McCain and stuck a finger in that eye, to crush the little viper that had been taunting me?

I had been such an easy target that night, and I did really feel targeted, amorphous and passive, as inert as a bull's-eye, incurably material.

And you knew it, Colter, and you too, Shannon and Harry, you all knew that things could take a turn like that at any moment; and you seemed to accept it, like a law of nature. Like something that had been in the making for eons.

And what about Moses, who didn't even stick his nose out to see what was going on, who stayed inside, at his bar, doing what, waiting for it all to be over; was he thinking that it was partially my own damn fault?

That was Moses's view on the matter, it was everyone's view: I had no business being there.

I'd overstayed my welcome, by a mile.

I'd thought I'd be able to settle into the *Ulysses* and find a place, but I was fooling myself. And I should have known that if I kept playing with fire, I'd eventually end up duking it out with someone—and not, that's the thing I should have figured out much earlier, with Colter, Shannon and Harry Dean, who had spent too much time with me at the bar for them to confront me directly, that they would be perfectly happy to leave the dirty work to someone else, a third party, because that's the way life goes, isn't it?

If only this whole story had nothing to do with me, but it does, because it's mine. I was the one who got his lights punched out, there beneath the American sky, by a McCain bodyguard who worked methodically to make it last, not too hard, not too fast. So that I'd get the lesson through my thick skull.

The wind's bitter taste, the rumbling of the waves, invisible from the street, that shred of cloud that would veil and unveil the moon like a tattered curtain waving in the night air, or an aging stripper in the back of some seedy bar where no one nourishes any illusions: and me, standing there with the beer in my belly weighing more than what I had ingurgitated, expanding into my whole body, distending my stomach; but it wasn't just that. Something else had me riveted in place.

We were panting by the end, and the fog of our breath showed sharp-edged in the low light, gray vapor in the cold night—there we were, him and me, two dragons, I thought, for although my body was fading fast, I was still able to formulate a number of thoughts.

The rest got pretty ugly.

At some point (and this might be a reconstruction after the fact), at some point, I seem to remember a dog barking in a nearby garden, then another joined in and still another, garden to garden, a canine commentary on what was going on.

You could sense their mounting excitement, not sure whether they were barking to intensify the brawl or to make it stop.

It's as if they were covering for the silence of all the other men who stood there staring, eyes glazed.

How far would it go, the bruises, the fractures, the broken ribs, my gut, at some point, they didn't seem to care anymore.

The wind was picking up on the beach, and its breeze sought me out.

I'm not going to tell you about the blood, the busted lip, the eyes swollen shut, the black and the blue, I really don't want to go there, and the sand stuck all over me, and my torn clothes. I had to get myself up somehow (maybe the TV image of the ambulance crew at the stadium crossed my mind just then, the wounded lying on the bleachers that they would then slip onto their stretchers, that day at the Blueberry, a day that seemed to contain the seeds of everything that was to follow, a day where everybody knew, one way or another, that this is what would happen in the end).

I still had the whole way to walk back to the motel, a trip that would take some time in my diminished state, requiring multiple stops, leaning against a wall to gather my strength and let the stabbing pain pass.

But I hadn't made up my mind to leave just yet.

I stayed a while longer, still groggy, seated uncomfortably on the wet sand, not so much ruminating over the fight and their non-intervention (my abandonment) as taking advantage of this last chance. Through the slits of my swollen eyes, I saw what I could of the sky, its carefree reverberations on the ground, where this vast expanse of sand looked like velvet. I was permeated by the beach, which, at dawn, felt bizarrely gentle (low tide, sounds in the distance, only a murmur, sand soft and tender).

The Room

I DON'T LEAVE the motel at all anymore.

All my days, all my nights are spent in this room, sleeping and watching the ocean.

The room I occupy, number 105, I could describe with my eyes shut. To the right of the door, you have the kitchenette. The melamine laminate cupboard contains three unmatched plates, each with a history of its own, next to three mismatched coffee mugs (one bears the name of some town, the other someone's first name, the third just says *Coffee*, in other words, three different lifestyle concepts for a damn coffee mug), though the Pyrex water glasses all seem to come from a single lot, neatly identical. A jar holding cafeteria cutlery sits on the narrow countertop next to the two blackened (or rusted?) electric heating elements, beneath which a small refrigerator well past its prime, dutiful but sweetly senile, fulfills its purpose against all odds (you feel its flimsiness when the door trembles and yawns every time the motor kicks in).

Turn around, and you're facing the picture window (the view is unbelievably spectacular), but you haven't seen the two mahogany benches and the tiny square table, built into the wall like train booths used to be. Then try to picture a lamp with a crooked shade poised above it, and the light it casts once night has come, duplicated in the windowpane, triangular, emitting a yellowish glow. You'll have to admit that the overall sensation is rather unpleasant, with the deep darkness outside and your plate beneath the lamplight, and the feeling of isolation takes on a bitter, acidic taste.

Anyone else would have been out of there a long time ago.

Because there is no shortage of reasons not to stick around, that's for sure.

Fear of retaliation, in case any of them felt I hadn't yet learned my lesson. Or the feeling I'd been deceived, and the word isn't strong enough to say what it meant to get beat up in front of Colter, Shannon, and Harry Dean, while they just stood and watched. Even the word *disillusioned* can't really get the feeling across.

I'd sympathized with them, listening to their stories night after night, stories I'd carried around with me: and they just stood there and watched, both feet planted in the ground, stiff and expressionless beneath the darkened sky. They simply spectated, as McCain's man made a punching bag out of the Frenchman under the hazy moon; they might as well have been at a boxing match, for all their reluctance to intervene and put a stop to it. They were like the posts of a boxing ring, framing the scene with their hollow, upright bodies, completely absent the way you sometimes get in moments of acute reality shock when, no matter how violent the event, you're strangely paralyzed by the notion of its inevitability. And that was the idea that bound them together, like the ropes around a boxing ring strung from one pole to the next, the thought that things had to unfold the way they did.

Every blow drove home the idea that I would never return to Moses's bar. That I'd never again enter those four dank walls and listen to their tales of woe. That night, my mouth full of blood, the bitter taste of final things.

If I haven't left Cannon Beach, I don't think it's out of pride (how proud could I feel after all that?). I'm not trying to prove to myself (or to them either, for that matter) that no one can tell me what I can or can't do. Nor is it that I don't want to feel like I'm running away, no, not because of a fear of fleeing. In fact, I'm perfectly at ease with that idea of fleeing.

It's because this is where I belong. It's something I can feel deep inside. I am in this room, and there is no other possible place in the whole world for me.

Outside the window, the ocean is playing out its stormily grandiose spectacle.

It's as if I've never known anything but this particular seascape. This grand iridescent fabric undulating beneath the boundless sky. I don't remember a time when I ever saw anything but this, the movement of water, the foam, the swelling and ebbing, in endless repetition, beneath the American skies.

The ocean's incessant sweep across the beach, rubbing the sand, then rubbing it again, seems to have erased entire eras from my memory. As if that were one of the ocean's duties, one of the tide's functions, to wipe the shore clean, a kind of cleansing amnesia, over time.

Because of the double-glazed windows, I can't hear the ocean from inside the room.

Someone hit the mute button on the ocean from here.

The anger is visible, but it's a silent movie.

All that bizarre, over-the-top violence, but without the sound of the violence.

Everything that goes into the ordinary soundtrack of windswept beaches, the blowing and crashing that adds to the frenzy, but which only makes sense when overlaid on the image, the sound you come to expect, natural, in direct proportion with geophysical and meteorological events; but from where I sit, nothing but the visuals, the naked spectacle of moving waves, and the white froth, like the ocean foaming at the mouth.

Nothing. Except, at regular intervals, in the thick, mind-numbing silence, the familiar sound of the refrigerator motor kicking in, wheezing and labored, as if to assure me it's still working, groveling for my favor (there's something fawning about the way refrigerator motors click on, I think). When it happens, I can't help thinking that it's at least a presence, a reassuring hum, to keep me company—and I blame myself for letting things come to this.

Here, No Ashes, No Soot, No Woodpile

I SPEND THE better part of my time stretched out on the king-size bed, or in a roomy armchair with its matching footrest, in front of the TV that, when turned off, creates an anamorphic reflection of the room, like the convex mirror of a Dutch painting.

In front of the fireplace, too, because the picture wouldn't be complete if I didn't say something about the fireplace.

A real piece of work, this fireplace.

Let's start with the mantelpiece. Who do they think they're fooling with this ersatz millstone look held together with cement? It couldn't be more obvious that the thing's been cast. A piece trying to pass for something belonging to the colonial era, I guess.

The hearth proper consists of a steel casing faced with heat-resistant tiles that create a fake masonry look. A fiction of logs is set in a studied, immutable jumble. Fiberglass embers scattered here and there complete the faux tableau.

What actually produces the flames (which are real, thankfully) is nothing but a gas jet. You need only flip the switch located to the right side of the fireplace to light the lovely, odorless flickering of flame.

Now, when I light the fire (not with the switch, but with a remote device, without even getting out of bed) and watch the clean, scrupulously even flames that rise in the hearth, never changing shape, strictly standardized, and lacking all initiative, I sometimes think of how much I used to enjoy watching the discrepant, indecisive, and unpredictable flames of a genuine wood fire. The power and glory of real flame, wild, oxygen-fueled and gaining strength from the updraft, the incandescent spectacle of it all. A catastrophe of sorts, as the dwindling log finally collapses noisily, shattered, defeated. And the ever-present danger of a flying spark (the blackened fire screen shielding the room beyond with its fragile metallic net); and a heat so intense that when you get too close, your cheeks glow red, and you feel the burn, a vague pain, but you don't mind. What makes you want it so, I wonder?

You set the logs on the andirons, and then, no, wait a second, aren't they a little too this way or that way (maybe a bit wet: beneath the tarp you threw over the woodpile dampness seeped in and took great delight in turning the logs into a soggy heap), and you wonder whether it's going to take now? You crouch down in front of the fireplace and hope for the best. You wad up a couple pages of newsprint and shove it under the wood, you know the technique, then light a match: the paper burns easily (as does the kindling, not to forget the kindling), but will the logs catch? Despite your hunkered position (your quads should be aching at this point), you stay down a while more, tongs in hand, trying to look the part. Sometimes you grab the log and shift its position, just a bit to the left, there you go, or here, let's center it; does any of this really matter? You could also try a few more wads of paper, the fast burn is gratifying but ephemeral. It's always something of a challenge, lighting a fire, for us city slickers, accustomed as we are to the convenience of central heating. Hoping it will make a difference, you grab a rustic old bellows (goatskin and beech wood with brass fixtures) that happens to be lying around and, still crouching in front of the hearth, you pump air through the accordion belly, puff-puff-puff, aiming the tip where you think the fire most likely to finally catch.

But here in my room, no ashes, no soot, no woodpile out in the yard, moldering away beneath the tarp, where you go out to get your logs in all kinds of wintry weather, icy sleet, or hail or fragile snowflakes drifting down that melt on contact with your warm body, soaking into your jacket (not to mention the splinters that the logs might lodge in the pulp of your thumb): the sales catalogs all agree, you won't regret your purchase of a gas-fueled fireplace.

Either that, or you need one of those backward-looking, old-timey temperaments that yearn for the way things used to be, and wax perpetually nostalgic: but let's face it, America isn't cut out for nostalgia.

So, those are the flames that warm me as night closes in on the ocean, when there's nothing left outdoors but a dark, inscrutable vastness, with an occasional glimmer off the foam. Sure-fingered, I press the squishy gray button on the remote, which makes contact with whatever electronic data set has been programmed to send an invisible message through the air of the room to the gas burner, which immediately springs to life, obeying my command.

The gas output is constant, you don't have to do anything, these gadgets work all by themselves, and I find something oddly comforting about the flames that consume the fuel at their own pace without my having to keep watch. A well-behaved flame that does what it's told and never lets me down (disappointment being a luxury I can ill afford).

A tidy little flame that doesn't consume anything at all. Not like those hungry, determined flames that devour and contort as they eat away at the log, doggedly, not realizing that by killing the log, reducing it to ashes, they'll die with it: nothing of that mighty struggle between fire and wood, where the fire, by savagely destroying the thing that feeds it, foolishly expires by its own criminal hand. Just an even stream of gas through a jet, sparked and lit by the burner, that will continue to flow so long as the switch is in the on position, reliable and professional.

No unforeseen episodes.

A uniform, calming spectacle that precludes any idea of surprise or event.

Maybe that's what I'm looking for after all.

What Do Salt Workers Think about While the Salt Is Slowly Crystallizing?

THE CLOSER THEY get to the end of their expedition, the more keenly the Lewis and Clark men long for home. The shorter the wait, the more impatient they become.

They strike out at dawn, walk through the dew that clings to their shoes like pearls. In the evening, they still have the strength to sing. But they are crazy with impatience, and isn't there something else working at cross purposes, if we listen more closely, something clashing with the liveliness that quickens the step? What is this bizarre dispiritedness, this reluctance, this doubt that is undermining their will? When a break in the weather allows them to resume their march to the ocean, now so tantalizingly close, their bodies move forward but aren't their souls secretly dragging their feet?

Once, Lewis thinks he hears the sound of waves crashing onto the rocky shore, or was it Clark, the rushing sound of water on rocks that they mistake for the ocean.

But it was not the ocean yet.

And again, the rain, clothing clinging to the skin, nights spent rotting away in the damp. They sleep on the riverbanks. Because of the tides, the next morning, they find their canoes full of water and have to bail.

They bail.

The water still looks too dangerous for them to resume their trek.

You'd think the ocean were denying them access.

It's right there, within reach, but getting to it is another matter.

And then one day it appears before them, the same one that swells behind the picture window of my room, that took them so many seasons to reach.

The Pacific Ocean, with all its seismic faults, its precariously balanced tectonic plates and ring of fire, a geographical misnomer, this ocean (thought Clark) (or was it Lewis), a surging sea that spared none.

They had so longed to finally arrive, and then, once they were standing before it, if we are to believe what we read, there was not a single cry of surprise, no one marveled: only technical issues mattered by then. But no one wrote anything about the shock of seeing the ocean with their own eyes. All Clark explains was that they set up camp at a certain distance from the beach, as the shoreline looks precarious to him.

Time to get organized.

A small band of men handle the salt-making, they are the salt workers. Others hunt, slogging through thickets in search of game that's playing hard to get. It isn't rare for them, unfortunately, to return empty-handed, their game bags flopping shapeless at their sides.

Some suggest they set traps, why not at least try, carefully camouflaged. You see them gauging the terrain, scratching their heads, positing the possible trajectories of their potential victims, delving into the animal mindset, studying their tastes and habits, oh look, some paw prints, and over here, a broken branch. They return later to check them, and in a great boost to their pride, they occasionally find their reasoning has been sound and their snares have delivered the goods.

If by goods, you mean the tattered remains of a raccoon, or so think those who favor gathering over hunting (though the pickings are slim in these areas swept by the ocean winds).

You can take it from me, just because you've reached the ocean, it doesn't mean the rain has stopped. Their return trip will have to wait.

They've had just about all they can stand of the great outdoors.

They continue to grumble about the rotten weather.

They made their salt in large pots, placing the seawater on low heat to evaporate the liquid and leave behind the salt.

It takes time.

Days and nights during which they keep watch and wait.

What do the salt workers think about while the salt is slowly crystallizing?

During the trek out to the Oregon territory, the ocean was foremost in their minds, but at present, they are naturally obsessed by the idea of homecoming. That moment when they cross the threshold of their little abode, which they have all but forgotten, a blurry daydream by now, fraught with all sorts of uncertainty.

They try to picture the bodies that will rise and rush toward them, the faces of those who will greet them, faces whose features have not only faded over time, but have continued to change in their absence, while their own faces have grown older, whipped by the wind, exposed to the elements, hardening in self-defense, their skin grown leathery and furrows grown deeper from straining into the gusts.

Oh, such a great distance from east to west, separating you from kith and kin. You'd love to be out of there, far from the ocean's cacophony. You try not to think, to simply carry out orders as best you can, to move along in the flow of time.

And that's what they do, the Lewis and Clark men.

The days seem identical, time stands still, but the cycle of nature wheels imperceptibly until the moment arrives for you to leave those desolate shores and return home.

Still, it doesn't matter how busy they are, little ants doing what they're told, crouching behind shore grass to hunt waterfowl, patching their tarps and whittling new tent stakes, repairing their gear that has degraded over time, like everything, like themselves, their bodies exhausted from weather and work, something in their hearts has worn out, too.

They aren't sure what that something is. They drag their feet along the sandy soil, eyes combing the ground for traces of some wild game, and they wonder at this new bitterness they're feeling.

Has their life in the outdoors reached its saturation point? Are they sick of nature, of the effort it asks of them, so dizzying, do they yearn for the volume of a house, the solidity of walls, the sound of feet on wooden floors, the footsteps of loved ones? Is it the acute longing for home that has taken the place of curiosity, and their dismay at the realization that the return trip will take them as many months as the journey out?

The faces of their near and dear are so fuzzy now: doesn't it seem as if they are locked forever in the present tense of this expedition? And once they are back together with their families, won't they have to reinvent the familiar, rediscover their old words? Those who've stayed behind under a roof for all that time, will they be capable of understanding anything about the two years the expedition men have just experienced? The pot hanging in the hearth, potatoes simmering with a little pork lard, filling the room with that familiar aroma, the table set for dinner, the warm, dry bed where one can lie down without fearing a midnight visit from a bear: that's where they spent their months without you, so how are they going to begin to conceive of dark forests, incessant rain, inescapable dampness that seeps into everything, the taste of otter meat, or that of your own horses that you had to put down when there was nothing else left to eat?

Back home, you'll sit around and reminisce about the days spent paddling your fragile canoes and nights spent under leaky tents, the vast skies above, and the rest, what will you do with that, once it's all over?

For there's a knack to going home.

Rediscovering the comfort of an armchair, remembering how to fit your body into its soft embrace.

No longer struggling to stay fed, dreaming of food.

No more winds uprooting trees, no more waves overturning your boats in the riverbed: the outdoors will now consist of the streets between narrow houses, and walking will involve moving between the facades, the horizon delineated by the village rooftops.

The food issue seems to be over now. Indians are selling them dried fish and wappatoo roots—don't ask me what those are. Out on the beach, flounder and sturgeon thrown onto the beach by the waves were there for the collecting, no fishing required. A bit further afield, over by the ponds, the elk that came to drink there will provide plentiful meat for all, and ducks fly overhead in great numbers. Plovers are caught and roasted over a camp-fire. The men will get by.

They carve their names into trees, with the date.

They sense things drawing to a close.

The Whale

FROM HERE, THE ocean is all you see.

Sometimes, I'd swear it's alive.

Once you've spent a certain amount of time by yourself, you start understanding what's around you in a way you wouldn't normally have.

I've really come to know it now: its moods, its habits of mind, its enthusiasms. By now, after staring for so long into its heaving mass, observing its convulsions, imagining its dark thoughts, its bitter, rancorous attitudes, all that cantankerous animosity, I think I can safely say it holds no secrets. I now can relate to how much anger it must take to move that much water and hurl it that far onto land, and then, still foaming at the mouth, accept defeat and retreat from the shore, only to make a comeback, and settle for slowly eating away at the rocks, so very gradually redesigning the coastline, when what it'd really like to do is to carry it all out to sea at one go. I've seen its rage explode when the waves crash onto the shore, like some furious act of vengeance, the righting of a wrong. This perpetual state of conflict with sand and rock, this need to draw a line in the sand and cross it, to feign defeat only to resurge glorious and renewed, a cycle of strategies, a war of attrition.

I've seen it coming, from far away and long ago.

Here's the story I tell myself. This creeping water mass inching forward, occasionally rising from its knees to its full, awesome height, isn't it like a kind of frothing, gray-green dragon that loathes our petty human existence just as it detests its own con-

195

dition, so adept at shape-shifting with the tidal movement, but lacking the drive to wrest itself from the perimeters enclosing it. Because that's what this watery monster really wants, as it keeps trying to get purchase, lifting itself, attempting to rise further but falling back onto the beach before retreating and starting over; and in its gasp, its final wheeze that I can't hear from where I sit but know so well, in that death rattle, you can hear the effort, all the pain involved in constant retraction and extension (I mean, look at all that saliva), the determination and despair, in the perpetual return of the tides. So, that's how I explain things, the ocean's hidden agenda, this body of water that stretches beneath the vast, unforgiving skies, its unfulfilled desire, this is the way I tell its story, I picture it as a single creature hoisting itself onto land: not to submerge it in increments, hit-or-miss, the way it usually behaves, or not just by isolated mega-waves, walls of water that devour a town or two, random strikes, lame vengeance, vain compensation for being nothing but a discontinuous, unstable and disorganized entity, no reparations will do; but for the whole damn thing to rise all at once, to cease its scattershot method of swallowing up whatever it happens upon (the ocean being omnivorous, it's true, gulping down the flesh of humans, the metal of cargo ships and the wood of rowboats, but if you were to ask, it would express a predilection for water, ever more water to swell its girth, expand its borders, take up more room), sucking up lakes, ponds and every little puddle on its way. Rivers are already pulled toward it, as we know, it draws them in like giant spaghetti strands; and as for all the standing water it hasn't yet accessed, it would go and gather it up in its soggy paws. And here's what follows: as you might have guessed, everything on earth dries up, nothing left but empty riverbeds, desiccated springs, vanished waterfalls whose rocky supports, still bearing the mark of water's passage, now lie exposed, baking in the sun. In the end, nothing will remain but sand and crackled earth, iron and concrete. And the water dragon, standing amidst all this devastation, will start suffering from heat exhaustion. It will search in vain for any sign of moisture, but the water table has dried up, as have the springs, and the thin trickles of what remained of the great waterfalls, so that the water dragon itself will begin to evaporate into the hot, dry air, losing volume day after day, hour after hour, until drought has absorbed the final droplet.

But until then, the ocean stays within its confines, biding its time as it shrinks and dilates, channeling algae and plankton, beaching the occasional asphyxiated fish.

And once, Lewis and Clark tell the story, just once, a whale.

So, here's the story of the whale.

They're sleepwalking through their daily drill, the routine having become so automatic by then, their thoughts in neutral; then the word spreads that there's a beached whale down on the shore.

Excitement ensues, all men as if at battle stations: at camp, a small group forms and decides to go have a look at the remains. They get into their canoes, put into the estuary and head for the ocean. In addition to their scientific curiosity, no sense denying it, they were also looking forward to the possibility of a meal or two.

They land the canoes and continue on foot. On their way, they pass the salt workers and hail them, all is well, it seems.

Yes, until their path is obstructed by a mass of boulders, too spikey and slippery to climb over. The only alternative, in my view, is to make a detour around the mountain. Let's do it, then, and they set out on the switchback trail that makes it possible to climb the steep hillside, as they try not to look down the vertiginous slope, keeping their eyes on their shoes.

They make it to the top, breathless but with a sense of accomplishment. Especially because the view, even though that's not why they made the climb, is truly gratifying: they exclaim at the beauty of the ocean panorama, the waves tossed passionately onto the shore, the ocean's tormented splendor whose dramatic vista contrasts with the verdant meadows nearby; it would have been a shame to miss this. Clark is exalting, and while he is at it, gives the place the name "Clark's Point of View." Something so delightful about leaving your name at a place you've passed through.

They still have to descend the other side. At times, the slope is so steep they have to walk sideways, like crabs. They take tiny steps, one at a time, hunched down at ground level. They look like ancient old men on some pilgrimage, legs shaky, steps unsure, eyes fixed to the ground slipping out from under them.

Finally, the sand, and there's the beached giant.

In truth, apart from a few strips of flesh still remaining on the bones, there's really nothing left but the carcass. Enormous white bones exposed to the blue sky. And in their ears, the noisy presence of the ocean reminds them of what had lifted this whale and placed it onto the shore. To what end, Clark wonders? You never know what the ocean might be up to. An offering or a warning?

The men stare into the animal's splayed entrails, their thoughts seizing at the sight, their minds reeling as the image of that gigantic skeleton is imprinted on their retinas.

Once over the initial shock, they return to earth. They weigh the practicality of trying to salvage anything from the whale remains; they set about cutting away whatever there is to cut, and from that, set aside anything edible or usable, in other words, they once again go about the business of survival on this far western American shore.

Standing at some distance, Clark, who isn't getting his hands dirty, is now pacing. He can't help but think of Jonah, and he thanks his lucky stars that they were sent a whale to eat instead of being eaten by one.

The men slice, dissect, and pile, while he gets completely wrapped up in that story, the story of Jonah who, with the flotsam and jetsam that had found its way into the whale's stomach, managed to fashion himself a chair and table, probably a bed, too, setting up house inside, for want of an alternative, living his days within the viscous, windowless walls. And there he was, waiting for what, exactly, just passing the time. He was even able to light some sort of oil lamp to ward off the gloom. He was a resourceful sort, a proto-Robinson Crusoe, if you will, who cobbled together his own little world, because you only have one life to live, and it's nice if you can make it last.

Home Sweet Home

ALL THIS WOULD eventually come to an end, of course. And the whole adventure would soon be nothing but a store of memories to recall back home by the fireside.

But for the moment, they were still there, and the bad weather had them stuck by the ocean, which they could see from their campsite, attracting their gaze with an almost magnetic force. The same ocean I've been watching for days now, my own private viewing as it continues to do its fancy dance out there, frothing up a storm, all that air and water whipped together just to get our attention, in the grip of some hysteria or other; not a presence you can get over easily.

It's alive and thundering, and that's what I'm dealing with here, this jelly-bellied beast, this evil, lumbering, uncontrollable, tireless behemoth. Constant companion, growling at my side, and thank heaven the window's there to keep us apart.

Swimming? No, I don't think that I dream I'm swimming.

Do I see myself facing an oncoming wave, rolling with it as it churns, or is it only the thought of water hitting the sand, the confrontation of ocean and shore, their endless combat?

I feel ballasted, actually. Like a big, fat barrel lifted and pounded by the waves of life in all its bleakness.

Here's another story I sometimes tell myself, about one of the henchmen that starts losing it, who gets more emotional than the others, because of some personal story going back to his childhood that makes him more attached to McCain than the

others, and who, for the same reason, would more likely rebel
against him. An adopted son of sorts, you know the kind, the
one you invest all your hopes in, and who, for fear of letting you
down, turns his weapon on you. To finally put an end to your
unrealizable expectations, the overwhelming pressure they exert.

I can picture him up there now, secretly plotting his
vengeance, what he calls his vengeance, without having any
clear idea of what he's about to avenge, apart from all that
affection he doesn't know how to return.

I force myself to think about this story of McCain's adopted son,
the basis for my tale. Bob is what I've called him, just to myself,
out of convenience, a short, rapid-fire name, like the bullet he'll
shoot into McCain's gut if they don't keep an eye on him.

I imagine him chafing up there in McCain's house, waiting
for his moment. He oils his gun, raises an eyebrow to the drizzly
outdoors, paces around the yard, has a smoke, irons a crease
into his trouser legs, and while he's performing these chores, all
sorts of thoughts are banging around in that thick skull.

Am I hoping that his act will make up for what I suffered?

To tell the truth, though, I don't think I'm really in the mood to
be making up much of anything.

I gaze out onto the empty beach, it looks exhausted by the
corrosive action of the ocean, passive, recumbent beneath the
pounding surf. I look at all that, and I say: that's me, that inert
sand, beaten senseless by the waves, in disbelief at the drubbing;
I've also given up, I believe. I'm resigned, vegetating, that's all,
present and void.

Lewis and Clark's men still have the wherewithal to see what's
around them, but it's not like it used to be, not the way it felt
when they were first setting out, keen for discovery and adventure. Their eyes have lost their sparkle, lids are drooping now,

but they still give it their best, with the idea that everything
they do feeds the stock of memories, since, at this point, they
have but one objective: to turn all this quotidian present into
the historic past.

To live long enough so that everything they're experiencing—
the rain that gullies the ground, their damp camping quarters,
their ragged clothing hanging out to dry whenever the thinnest
ray of sunlight breaks through the clouds, the towering ocean
waves—all that should be reduced to nothing but mind
pictures floating in the warmth of hearth and home, haunting
the memories of men sitting in those same armchairs they had
abandoned years before. This is what keeps them going, the
thought that all this present, as painful and palpable as it is,
will one day be nothing but the fluid, intangible stuff of reverie.

Sometimes, they stand before the ocean, legs spread for better
balance, hands like visors shading their eyes. What are they
wishing? For the silhouette of a supply ship coming to replenish
their vanished stocks. When they go down to the beach or gaze
out at the water from a promontory, they squint and scan the
seas for just that, the unlikely outline of a ship with a hull full
of all kinds of foodstuffs. That's what they're all on the lookout
for, that dark dot on the horizon, that tiny object that will
grow larger as it draws nearer, and soon be positively identified,
beyond a shadow of a doubt.

But I don't believe that ship ever did sail into view.

So, they chew away at their gamey moose meat, the little sturgeon or anchovy they're able to catch, as they gaze mournfully
heavenward at the uniform gray tent of clouds.

And then, two or three signs that spring can't be far off.

Out on a walk, Lewis sees a blueberry bush starting to sprout
leaves.

They would set out for home the next day.

It's hard to say what it felt like for these men to get back into their canoes, leaving their winter quarters, and to start back upstream.

The water was choppy because of the tides, and it was hardly smooth sailing, but hallelujah, the rains that had imprisoned them for months had finally let up, the wait was over, the pointless delays a thing of the past. They were on the move again. The riverbanks scrolled past, and every yard they clicked off brought them closer to home sweet home. Even the rocking of their boats felt good to them, for wasn't it imitating their beating hearts ready to capsize with joy.

The skies did their part, with the sun tearing through the cloud layer and lighting up the estuary. The light came in thick, nebulous rays, pouring out of the sky in oblique columns, giving the landscape an otherworldly feel, as if something up there were about to speak. The men of the expedition saw this, and their hearts soared like, I don't know, maybe an operatic aria.

The Queen Termite

Settle into my armchair, set your forearms on its wide armrests, let your ankles relax on the footrest: isn't there something about this chair that calls you to vegetate?

That was it, the call of the armchair. From the very first time I entered the room and saw the empty beach through the picture window, the king-size bed, the fake fireplace, and that huge armchair with upholstery so dark it absorbed all thought, here's what the chair was saying, which I couldn't understand back then, the crazy thought that crossed my mind, but that I dismissed as crackpot: just like the dead body of the beached whale found by the expedition that I had never even heard of back then, that huge whale whose carcass they found on the beach, I was going to run aground here, at Cannon Beach, in this motel room, watching the light change, obsessed by the tidal evacuation, vindicated by the water's pigheadedness from ever getting personally involved in anything at all.

Something in me knew, as soon as I walked through the door that dragged noisily over the olive green carpet as I entered, when I raised the blinds and saw the waves, and saw the blanket folded up on the chair, and once I'd made sure the gas jet worked properly when I pressed the button to the right of the phony fireplace: I knew, but pretended not to, and stretched out on the bedspread to rest my bones after the long road.

Ever since I locked myself away in this room, completely idle in this motel on America's far western shore, eating only the local fare—pizzas and hamburgers that I have delivered—my body has become American.

This must be what I was looking for, this metamorphosis.

And you have to admit, with all this space around you, and I don't only mean the idea of space, though it is also an idea, with the notion of thousands and thousands of square miles under such endlessly vast skies, you can understand how living in such an expanse of territory would make you want to acquire girth. To take up more room in this vastness. To try to somehow measure up, proportionately, to the hugeness of the place.

Put simply, to adapt your body size to the landscape's dimensions.

It's hard to get around, weighed down by all this extra flesh, and I sometimes get the strange feeling that I'm at the center of some enormous device that I am attempting to control remotely, and that doesn't always respond appropriately to my commands.

But I see it as an opportunity for an enhanced presence, the satisfaction of occupying more room than I used to.

I carried so little weight, before.

I took up so little space in the midst of everything else.

The blanket pulled up to my sternum, I gaze at the ocean, aware of my new proportions, and I delight in my staggering corporality.

This is how the queen termite must feel, too. Something in her that is both sprawling and royal. All those tiny insects that keep her clean, as she wallows in her enormousness, in her bulging folds, her white skin, stretched to nearly bursting, her resemblance to a length of swollen intestine, a life summed up by eating and expanding.

It's like an augmentation of my being. I look at myself and say: I'm all that.

My memories must have gotten diluted by all this fat, lost in folds of flesh. My face turned toward the interminable ocean and the wide-open sky, my past life is now a blank.

I sometimes believe I'm about to recall something, but then, no. There's a certain momentum, a sense of forward motion, and then it falls back again. It's the movement that memories make inside you as they try to emerge, the early phase of that movement—but that's as far as it goes. The first quivering of a restlessness within, then nothing, in the end, but the quivering.

But if I did have any memories, this is how I explain it, I'd see a lean man with a light, supple step, who would walk, la-di-da, as if on air. I'd see him skipping about and wonder: who is that fleet-footed wisp of a person that I see in this picture? It would be like watching someone else's adventure story.

The man I have become, the obese man, doesn't have a story yet.

His origin dates back to the day he rented the white Ford and drove out of Long Beach, California, where he was just passing through, after stopping a moment, you might recall, to watch the killer pelicans carry out their slaughter. The day he hit the road and drove, unbeknownst to him, toward his future proportions. When he got into the car, when he stopped at the Blueberry Inn, when he stepped into his room at the Waves Motel for the first time, he didn't look the way he does now. But his new body was in gestation. That was the day, I'm convinced of it, that the idea of this new appearance, a subterranean idea, had begun circulating deep within. As soon as that man, still fit enough, but with the idea beginning to do its work without his realizing it, as soon as that man opened the door to his room, he knew. He said to the hotel clerk, Yes, this will do for one night, but deep down, he knew.

It's something that was bound to happen (my reclusion, my onset of obesity), with or without Colter and the others.

At this point, I'm not even sure whether Colter and the gang ever even existed.

I sometimes wonder whether we ever crossed paths, back when I was still setting foot out the door. Or were they creatures I invented to keep me company, night after night, in the solitude of my room, as the evening chill settled on the windowpane and the monochrome seascape, which is all you could see, faded into twilight.

I'm not even sure about *Ulysses Returns*.

The main street of Cannon Beach, the grocery store, sure, I remember all that. The Blueberry Inn, before I got here, the chiliburger, Wendy, the three guys watching television, for sure, I swear that's all true.

But after that, whether there was a bar called *Ulysses Returns*, whether I met up with those same three guys again, whether their names were really Colter, Shannon, and Harry Dean, I wouldn't stake my life on it, no.

It's all become a slurry of dark dreams, I can't tell what's real anymore.

Nothing but the Waves and the Wind

THE LIGHT IS constantly changing here, the cloud patterns and the way they color the ocean, as if the outdoors were always worried about its personal appearance, forever trying on something new, endless versions of itself, never able to decide on any one look.

Dogs yapping on the beach, you can see the open-shut action of their maws, but the sound hits my window and stops. I think they must be yelps of joy, because dogs, even though they're on leashes, feel free somehow (go figure) when they're out in the wind.

Oh, and look, there's a kite, wavering in that infinite sky. The man at the other end is gripping the reel hard, attempting to steer the leading edge, his face upturned and focused on the restive, unruly flying object. His eyes riveted on the insubordinate thing, the man seems now powerless to control the fragile cloth flyer as it trembles in the turbulent air currents and does what it will, resisting orders, pulling harder and harder on the string in its effort to break free.

The man wishes he knew how to handle it more artfully, to put it through the catalogue of kite figures, but the kite has a mind of its own up there, balking at authority, shifting erratically; it occasionally dives earthward without warning, its face in the wet sand. The man picks it up, shakes off the sand—I sigh at the series of little fails beneath my window—and starts over. Why keep starting over?

Every once in a while, on this same beach, you'll see a crow that thinks it's a seagull.

Here's how it goes, simply put: a couple of guys in puffer jackets eating sandwiches as they stare out at the waves, and at their feet, a few begging seagulls in a waiting pattern, patiently focusing on the next crumb to be tossed their way, each bird preparing to outmaneuver the others and spring for the catch. And standing back a little ways, I kid you not, is our crow, all alone and tousled by the wind, looking like something that has just blown in from the uplands and is wondering what to do with all this sand, and all those waves coming at you: a weary traveler in a soiled overcoat wonders how it has landed in such a godforsaken place, feeling a little confused and insecure, hoping it will be able to somehow fit into the group.

Glancing down at its own plumage, it must certainly realize that it isn't exactly the same species as the others (and what does it think of their calls, not quite like its own?); but it does so want to be accepted. It's after the food, of course, but because the gulls are its only point of reference, it starts mimicking their behavior in the strangest way.

Cautious at first, observing from a distance the arc of the crumbs that reach the beak of this or that gull, it gains enough confidence to go join their ranks. It stands among them, looking overjoyed at the company, mirroring their behavior and doing a convincing imitation, completely at ease with its personality disorder, out there on the windy beach.

The only surprise comes when the others spread their wings and head out to sea, while it naturally chooses to return inland.

And on its way, it passes over the solitary kite-flyer who, tethered to his cloth-and-wire contraption that acts as a bizarre appendage at the end of its string, sends the kite into the sky like the part of himself capable of flight.

Scattered over the strand, the ubiquitous beachcombers with their dogs yanking on their leashes, yearning to break and run, pulling them forward, an odd coupling. The masters, their bodies leaning backward at an angle that I guess counteracts the dog's forward motion, slide by my window on their invisible sleds. And the sledding impression is even stronger when they are walking more than one dog at a time, like that man with three setters—remember him?—who comes out to walk them on the beach: the three of them are really pulling him along, and he's trying to dig in his heels, shouting Slow down, and Take it easy, but they aren't having any of it, and their flapping ears can hear nothing but the waves and the wind.

CHRISTINE MONTALBETTI is an award-winning novelist, essayist, critic and professor of literature at the University of Paris VIII. *Nothing but Waves and Wind* was inspired by a trip she took to Oregon, where the landscape fueled her imagination, and gave rise to a series of down-and-out characters whose violence and unpredictability seems determined by their surroundings.

JANE KUNTZ has translated nine works of fiction for Dalkey Archive Press. She holds a doctorate in Francophone Literature, and spent eighteen years in Tunisia. She now lives and works in Urbana, Illinois. Her most recent translation is *History of the Grandparents I Never Had*, by Ivan Jablonka (Stanford University Press, 2016).

MICHAL AJVAZ, *The Golden Age.*
The Other City.
PIERRE ALBERT-BIROT, *Grabinoulor.*
YUZ ALESHKOVSKY, *Kangaroo.*
FELIPE ALFAU, *Chromos.*
Locos.
JOE AMATO, *Samuel Taylor's Last Night.*
IVAN ÂNGELO, *The Celebration.*
The Tower of Glass.
ANTÓNIO LOBO ANTUNES, *Knowledge of Hell.*
The Splendor of Portugal.
ALAIN ARIAS-MISSON, *Theatre of Incest.*
JOHN ASHBERY & JAMES SCHUYLER, *A Nest of Ninnies.*
ROBERT ASHLEY, *Perfect Lives.*
GABRIELA AVIGUR-ROTEM, *Heatwave and Crazy Birds.*
DJUNA BARNES, *Ladies Almanack.*
Ryder.
JOHN BARTH, *Letters.*
Sabbatical.
DONALD BARTHELME, *The King.*
Paradise.
SVETISLAV BASARA, *Chinese Letter.*
MIQUEL BAUÇÀ, *The Siege in the Room.*
RENÉ BELLETTO, *Dying.*
MAREK BIENCZYK, *Transparency.*
ANDREI BITOV, *Pushkin House.*
ANDREJ BLATNIK, *You Do Understand.*
Law of Desire.
LOUIS PAUL BOON, *Chapel Road.*
My Little War.
Summer in Termuren.
ROGER BOYLAN, *Killoyle.*
IGNÁCIO DE LOYOLA BRANDÃO, *Anonymous Celebrity.*
Zero.
BONNIE BREMSER, *Troia: Mexican Memoirs.*
CHRISTINE BROOKE-ROSE, *Amalgamemnon.*
BRIGID BROPHY, *In Transit.*
The Prancing Novelist.

GERALD L. BRUNS, *Modern Poetry and the Idea of Language.*
GABRIELLE BURTON, *Heartbreak Hotel.*
MICHEL BUTOR, *Degrees.*
Mobile.
G. CABRERA INFANTE, *Infante's Inferno.*
Three Trapped Tigers.
JULIETA CAMPOS, *The Fear of Losing Eurydice.*
ANNE CARSON, *Eros the Bittersweet.*
ORLY CASTEL-BLOOM, *Dolly City.*
LOUIS-FERDINAND CÉLINE, *North.*
Conversations with Professor Y.
London Bridge.
MARIE CHAIX, *The Laurels of Lake Constance.*
HUGO CHARTERIS, *The Tide Is Right.*
ERIC CHEVILLARD, *Demolishing Nisard.*
The Author and Me.
MARC CHOLODENKO, *Mordechai Schamz.*
JOSHUA COHEN, *Witz.*
EMILY HOLMES COLEMAN, *The Shutter of Snow.*
ERIC CHEVILLARD, *The Author and Me.*
ROBERT COOVER, *A Night at the Movies.*
STANLEY CRAWFORD, *Log of the S.S.*
The Mrs Unguentine.
Some Instructions to My Wife.
RENÉ CREVEL, *Putting My Foot in It.*
RALPH CUSACK, *Cadenza.*
NICHOLAS DELBANCO, *Sherbrookes.*
The Count of Concord.
NIGEL DENNIS, *Cards of Identity.*
PETER DIMOCK, *A Short Rhetoric for Leaving the Family.*
ARIEL DORFMAN, *Konfidenz.*
COLEMAN DOWELL, *Island People.*
Too Much Flesh and Jabez.
ARKADII DRAGOMOSHCHENKO, *Dust.*
RIKKI DUCORNET, *Phosphor in Dreamland.*
The Complete Butcher's Tales.

RIKKI DUCORNET (cont.), *The Jade Cabinet.*

The Fountains of Neptune.

WILLIAM EASTLAKE, *The Bamboo Bed.*

Castle Keep.

Lyric of the Circle Heart.

JEAN ECHENOZ, *Chopin's Move.*

STANLEY ELKIN, *A Bad Man.*

Criers and Kibitzers, Kibitzers and Criers.

The Dick Gibson Show.

The Franchiser.

The Living End.

Mrs. Ted Bliss.

FRANÇOIS EMMANUEL, *Invitation to a Voyage.*

PAUL EMOND, *The Dance of a Sham.*

SALVADOR ESPRIU, *Ariadne in the Grotesque Labyrinth.*

LESLIE A. FIEDLER, *Love and Death in the American Novel.*

JUAN FILLOY, *Op Oloop.*

ANDY FITCH, *Pop Poetics.*

GUSTAVE FLAUBERT, *Bouvard and Pécuchet.*

KASS FLEISHER, *Talking out of School.*

JON FOSSE, *Aliss at the Fire.*

Melancholy.

FORD MADOX FORD, *The March of Literature.*

MAX FRISCH, *I'm Not Stiller.*

Man in the Holocene.

CARLOS FUENTES, *Christopher Unborn.*

Distant Relations.

Terra Nostra.

Where the Air Is Clear.

TAKEHIKO FUKUNAGA, *Flowers of Grass.*

WILLIAM GADDIS, JR., *The Recognitions.*

JANICE GALLOWAY, *Foreign Parts.*

The Trick Is to Keep Breathing.

WILLIAM H. GASS, *Life Sentences.*

The Tunnel.

The World Within the Word.

Willie Masters' Lonesome Wife.

GÉRARD GAVARRY, *Hoppla! 1 2 3.*

ETIENNE GILSON, *The Arts of the Beautiful.*

Forms and Substances in the Arts.

C. S. GISCOMBE, *Giscome Road.*

Here.

DOUGLAS GLOVER, *Bad News of the Heart.*

WITOLD GOMBROWICZ, *A Kind of Testament.*

PAULO EMÍLIO SALES GOMES, *P's Three Women.*

GEORGI GOSPODINOV, *Natural Novel.*

JUAN GOYTISOLO, *Count Julian.*

Juan the Landless.

Makbara.

Marks of Identity.

HENRY GREEN, *Blindness.*

Concluding.

Doting.

Nothing.

JACK GREEN, *Fire the Bastards!*

JIŘÍ GRUŠA, *The Questionnaire.*

MELA HARTWIG, *Am I a Redundant Human Being?*

JOHN HAWKES, *The Passion Artist.*

Whistlejacket.

ELIZABETH HEIGHWAY, ED., *Contemporary Georgian Fiction.*

AIDAN HIGGINS, *Balcony of Europe.*

Blind Man's Bluff.

Bornholm Night-Ferry.

Langrishe, Go Down.

Scenes from a Receding Past.

KEIZO HINO, *Isle of Dreams.*

KAZUSHI HOSAKA, *Plainsong.*

ALDOUS HUXLEY, *Antic Hay.*

Point Counter Point.

Those Barren Leaves.

Time Must Have a Stop.

NAOYUKI II, *The Shadow of a Blue Cat.*

DRAGO JANČAR, *The Tree with No Name.*

MIKHEIL JAVAKHISHVILI, *Kvachi.*

GERT JONKE, *The Distant Sound.*

Homage to Czerny.

The System of Vienna.

JACQUES JOUET, *Mountain R.*
Savage.
Upstaged.
MIEKO KANAI, *The Word Book.*
YORAM KANIUK, *Life on Sandpaper.*
ZURAB KARUMIDZE, *Dagny.*
JOHN KELLY, *From Out of the City.*
HUGH KENNER, *Flaubert, Joyce
and Beckett: The Stoic Comedians.*
Joyce's Voices.
DANILO KIŠ, *The Attic.*
The Lute and the Scars.
Psalm 44.
A Tomb for Boris Davidovich.
ANITA KONKKA, *A Fool's Paradise.*
GEORGE KONRÁD, *The City Builder.*
TADEUSZ KONWICKI, *A Minor
Apocalypse.*
The Polish Complex.
ANNA KORDZAIA-SAMADASHVILI,
Me, Margarita.
MENIS KOUMANDAREAS, *Koula.*
ELAINE KRAF, *The Princess of 72nd Street.*
JIM KRUSOE, *Iceland.*
AYSE KULIN, *Farewell: A Mansion in
Occupied Istanbul.*
EMILIO LASCANO TEGUI, *On Elegance
While Sleeping.*
ERIC LAURRENT, *Do Not Touch.*
VIOLETTE LEDUC, *La Bâtarde.*
EDOUARD LEVÉ, *Autoportrait.*
Newspaper.
Suicide.
Works.
MARIO LEVI, *Istanbul Was a Fairy Tale.*
DEBORAH LEVY, *Billy and Girl.*
JOSÉ LEZAMA LIMA, *Paradiso.*
ROSA LIKSOM, *Dark Paradise.*
OSMAN LINS, *Avalovara.*
The Queen of the Prisons of Greece.
FLORIAN LIPUŠ, *The Errors of Young Tjaž.*
GORDON LISH, *Peru.*
ALF MACLOCHLAINN, *Out of Focus.*
Past Habitual.

The Corpus in the Library.
RON LOEWINSOHN, *Magnetic Field(s).*
YURI LOTMAN, *Non-Memoirs.*
D. KEITH MANO, *Take Five.*
MINA LOY, *Stories and Essays of Mina Loy.*
MICHELINE AHARONIAN MARCOM,
A Brief History of Yes.
The Mirror in the Well.
BEN MARCUS, *The Age of Wire and String.*
WALLACE MARKFIELD, *Teitlebaum's
Window.*
DAVID MARKSON, *Reader's Block.*
Wittgenstein's Mistress.
CAROLE MASO, *AVA.*
HISAKI MATSUURA, *Triangle.*
LADISLAV MATEJKA & KRYSTYNA
POMORSKA, EDS., *Readings in Russian
Poetics: Formalist & Structuralist Views.*
HARRY MATHEWS, *Cigarettes.*
The Conversions.
The Human Country.
The Journalist.
My Life in CIA.
Singular Pleasures.
The Sinking of the Odradek.
Stadium.
Tlooth.
HISAKI MATSUURA, *Triangle.*
DONAL MCLAUGHLIN, *beheading the
virgin mary, and other stories.*
JOSEPH MCELROY, *Night Soul and
Other Stories.*
ABDELWAHAB MEDDEB, *Talismano.*
GERHARD MEIER, *Isle of the Dead.*
HERMAN MELVILLE, *The Confidence-
Man.*
AMANDA MICHALOPOULOU, *I'd Like.*
STEVEN MILLHAUSER, *The Barnum
Museum.*
In the Penny Arcade.
RALPH J. MILLS, JR., *Essays on Poetry.*
MOMUS, *The Book of Jokes.*
CHRISTINE MONTALBETTI, *The Origin
of Man.*
Western.

NICHOLAS MOSLEY, *Accident*.
Assassins.
Catastrophe Practice.
A Garden of Trees.
Hopeful Monsters.
Imago Bird.
Inventing God.
Look at the Dark.
Metamorphosis.
Natalie Natalia.
Serpent.
WARREN MOTTE, *Fables of the Novel: French Fiction since 1990*.
Fiction Now: The French Novel in the 21st Century.
Mirror Gazing.
Oulipo: A Primer of Potential Literature.
GERALD MURNANE, *Barley Patch*.
Inland.
YVES NAVARRE, *Our Share of Time*.
Sweet Tooth.
DOROTHY NELSON, *In Night's City*.
Tar and Feathers.
ESHKOL NEVO, *Homesick*.
WILFRIDO D. NOLLEDO, *But for the Lovers*.
BORIS A. NOVAK, *The Master of Insomnia*.
FLANN O'BRIEN, *At Swim-Two-Birds*.
The Best of Myles.
The Dalkey Archive.
The Hard Life.
The Poor Mouth.
The Third Policeman.
CLAUDE OLLIER, *The Mise-en-Scène*.
Wert and the Life Without End.
PATRIK OUŘEDNÍK, *Europeana*.
The Opportune Moment, 1855.
BORIS PAHOR, *Necropolis*.
FERNANDO DEL PASO, *News from the Empire*.
Palinuro of Mexico.
ROBERT PINGET, *The Inquisitory*.
Mahu or The Material.
Trio.
MANUEL PUIG, *Betrayed by Rita Hayworth*.

The Buenos Aires Affair.
Heartbreak Tango.
RAYMOND QUENEAU, *The Last Days*.
Odile.
Pierrot Mon Ami.
Saint Glinglin.
ANN QUIN, *Berg*.
Passages.
Three.
Tripticks.
ISHMAEL REED, *The Free-Lance Pallbearers*.
The Last Days of Louisiana Red.
Ishmael Reed: The Plays.
Juice!
The Terrible Threes.
The Terrible Twos.
Yellow Back Radio Broke-Down.
JASIA REICHARDT, *15 Journeys Warsaw to London*.
JOÃO UBALDO RIBEIRO, *House of the Fortunate Buddhas*.
JEAN RICARDOU, *Place Names*.
RAINER MARIA RILKE,
The Notebooks of Malte Laurids Brigge.
JULIÁN RÍOS, *The House of Ulysses*.
Larva: A Midsummer Night's Babel.
Poundemonium.
ALAIN ROBBE-GRILLET, *Project for a Revolution in New York*.
A Sentimental Novel.
AUGUSTO ROA BASTOS, *I the Supreme*.
DANIËL ROBBERECHTS, *Arriving in Avignon*.
JEAN ROLIN, *The Explosion of the Radiator Hose*.
OLIVIER ROLIN, *Hotel Crystal*.
ALIX CLEO ROUBAUD, *Alix's Journal*.
JACQUES ROUBAUD, *The Form of a City Changes Faster, Alas, Than the Human Heart*.
The Great Fire of London.
Hortense in Exile.
Hortense Is Abducted.
Mathematics: The Plurality of Worlds of Lewis.
Some Thing Black.

RAYMOND ROUSSEL, *Impressions of Africa.*

VEDRANA RUDAN, *Night.*

PABLO M. RUIZ, *Four Cold Chapters on the Possibility of Literature.*

GERMAN SADULAEV, *The Maya Pill.*

TOMAŽ ŠALAMUN, *Soy Realidad.*

LYDIE SALVAYRE, *The Company of Ghosts.*
The Lecture.
The Power of Flies.

LUIS RAFAEL SÁNCHEZ, *Macho Camacho's Beat.*

SEVERO SARDUY, *Cobra & Maitreya.*

NATHALIE SARRAUTE, *Do You Hear Them?*
Martereau.
The Planetarium.

STIG SÆTERBAKKEN, *Siamese.*
Self-Control.
Through the Night.

ARNO SCHMIDT, *Collected Novellas.*
Collected Stories.
Nobodaddy's Children.
Two Novels.

ASAF SCHURR, *Motti.*

GAIL SCOTT, *My Paris.*

DAMION SEARLS, *What We Were Doing and Where We Were Going.*

JUNE AKERS SEESE,
Is This What Other Women Feel Too?

BERNARD SHARE, *Inish.*
Transit.

VIKTOR SHKLOVSKY, *Bowstring.*
Literature and Cinematography.
Theory of Prose.
Third Factory.
Zoo, or Letters Not about Love.

PIERRE SINIAC, *The Collaborators.*

KJERSTI A. SKOMSVOLD,
The Faster I Walk, the Smaller I Am.

JOSEF ŠKVORECKÝ, *The Engineer of Human Souls.*

GILBERT SORRENTINO, *Aberration of Starlight.*
Blue Pastoral.
Crystal Vision.

Imaginative Qualities of Actual Things.
Mulligan Stew. Red the Fiend.
Steelwork.
Under the Shadow.

MARKO SOSIČ, *Ballerina, Ballerina.*

ANDRZEJ STASIUK, *Dukla.*
Fado.

GERTRUDE STEIN, *The Making of Americans.*
A Novel of Thank You.

LARS SVENDSEN, *A Philosophy of Evil.*

PIOTR SZEWC, *Annihilation.*

GONÇALO M. TAVARES, *A Man: Klaus Klump.*
Jerusalem.
Learning to Pray in the Age of Technique.

LUCIAN DAN TEODOROVICI,
Our Circus Presents . . .

NIKANOR TERATOLOGEN, *Assisted Living.*

STEFAN THEMERSON, *Hobson's Island.*
The Mystery of the Sardine.
Tom Harris.

TAEKO TOMIOKA, *Building Waves.*

JOHN TOOMEY, *Sleepwalker.*

DUMITRU TSEPENEAG, *Hotel Europa.*
The Necessary Marriage.
Pigeon Post.
Vain Art of the Fugue.

ESTHER TUSQUETS, *Stranded.*

DUBRAVKA UGRESIC, *Lend Me Your Character.*
Thank You for Not Reading.

TOR ULVEN, *Replacement.*

MATI UNT, *Brecht at Night.*
Diary of a Blood Donor.
Things in the Night.

ÁLVARO URIBE & OLIVIA SEARS, EDS.,
Best of Contemporary Mexican Fiction.

ELOY URROZ, *Friction.*
The Obstacles.

LUISA VALENZUELA, *Dark Desires and the Others.*
He Who Searches.

PAUL VERHAEGHEN, *Omega Minor.*

BORIS VIAN, *Heartsnatcher.*

LLORENÇ VILLALONGA, *The Dolls' Room.*

TOOMAS VINT, *An Unending Landscape.*

ORNELA VORPSI, *The Country Where No One Ever Dies.*

AUSTRYN WAINHOUSE, *Hedyphagetica.*

CURTIS WHITE, *America's Magic Mountain.*
The Idea of Home.
Memories of My Father Watching TV.
Requiem.

DIANE WILLIAMS,
Excitability: Selected Stories.
Romancer Erector.

DOUGLAS WOOLF, *Wall to Wall.*
Ya! & John-Juan.

JAY WRIGHT, *Polynomials and Pollen.*
The Presentable Art of Reading Absence.

PHILIP WYLIE, *Generation of Vipers.*

MARGUERITE YOUNG, *Angel in the Forest.*
Miss MacIntosh, My Darling.

REYOUNG, *Unbabbling.*

VLADO ŽABOT, *The Succubus.*

ZORAN ŽIVKOVIĆ , *Hidden Camera.*

LOUIS ZUKOFSKY, *Collected Fiction.*

VITOMIL ZUPAN, *Minuet for Guitar.*

SCOTT ZWIREN, *God Head.*

AND MORE . . .